CATCH
ONE CATCH
'EM ALL

by

FREDDIE JONES

Airedale Press

Copyright 2017 by Freddie Jones

ISBN: 10 - 0692127887
ISBN: 13 - 9780692127889

 Catch One Catch Em All

Dedication

This novel is dedicated to
Mrs. Dorothy Gregg
Scientist, Educator, Inspiration

PROLOGUE

We had no idea we were forming patterns that would shape the rest of our lives. For instance, many of the innocent little kiddie games we played were really based on serious adult themes like May Day at Mayo Elementary.

The whole school would turn out in the playground; shining little faces happy to be out of the classroom. There we'd find these tall wooden poles on pedestals set up (like flagpoles without the flags) with a lot of different colored crepe paper streamers hanging from the top of each one. With all the kids facing in one direction around the poles, every other kid turned around to face the kid behind him/her. When the music started we would parade happily around the "May Pole" taking our streamers over the first kid's streamer in front of them then under the next, thus creating a pretty cacophony of colors down the pole as the kids pranced round and round like a beautiful carousel umbrella. What a great time that was as we giggled and romped in the springtime sun.

Many years later I'd discover May Day was a pagan ceremony celebrating springtime fertility of the soil and women. The Maypole was a phallic symbol that we swam around like little spermatozoa worshiping this big dick of white male superiority. I guess eventually it was deemed politically incorrect and discontinued with a little smirk no doubt. What a gyp.

Anyway, there was this game we used to play called "Catch One Catch 'em All." It was essentially a game of 'Tag' starting with one person being 'it' who would chase the rest of us around eventually tagging someone who would then join him in chasing the others. Once those two tagged the third player, the three would go after another until everybody wound up chasing the one last elusive player.

First, the initial patsy was chosen by a foot race, meaning the slowest person would always lose thereby making the selection process inherently unfair. On top of that, he'd start the game winded from the sprint placing him at a disadvantage before he even began. This is a metaphor for the absurdity of life in that the weak are never nurtured but instead feasted upon so the strong might survive.

Once the initial patsy tags a runner, he (the tagged runner) goes after his comrades with whom he was only moments before in 'get-away' alliance. This is the very adult lesson of not getting too familiar with anyone lest they turn on you when it serves them to do so.

Ultimately, everyone is now after the last surviving runner who is set upon like an antelope on the Serengeti teeming with lions. This last brutal act is the coldest shot of all, mirroring the world in all its treacherous beauty. You can live your whole life smelling roses and avoiding potholes only to be consumed whole, out of breath, by the very society you'd frolicked in so freely your entire life.

A CHANCE AT TRAGEDY

We lived in a rat-infested tenement on Chicago's south side. I was one, my brother Corey was one month, and two others would come later. We slept together in a rickety old crib someone had given us. My mother and father were still together then and slept in an adjoining room. Most of the time it was just my mother and us because my father stayed out drunk a lot.

One night as Corey and I slept undoubtedly with milk breath and a few belated crumbs on unwashed faces, a fat assed rat climbed into the crib and sunk its teeth into my little brother. My mother was young and didn't know what to do so at twenty years old with no money and a drunk assed husband, she went to a fifteen dollar corner doctor who gave her some ointment and sent us back home. My brother died two days later never having seen as much as an emergency room.

As I think back on my ambiguous fortune and how easily it could have been me in that tiny roaster sized coffin, I can't help but wonder how Corey would have fared moving on to Chicago's Ida B. Wells Housing Project. On which side of the statistical fence would he have fallen in those pissy catacombs of poverty and hopelessness? It could have been me bitten by that rat. I could have swollen yellow with jaundice, a dripping balloon so infected that my eyes wouldn't close. It could have been me so deformed in only two days that the wake had to be a closed casket service; my mother fainting, no doubt filled with guilt. I was right there but the rat went for the younger, juicier flesh. No modest proposal as I reflect on God's will to endow me with a tragic encounter of ignominious proportions. I was spared to battle a whole gang of rats, bearing slavered fangs dripping with the venom of unrequited dreams. Every bad thing on earth was about to happen to me and the really sad part was that there was no poison I could lay down to ward it off.

THE MOVE WITHOUT DADDY

When my father raped the babysitter, that event along with his subsequent incarceration precipitated our move to the projects. The babysitter was a young girl maybe seventeen or eighteen who had been sleeping with a lot of the guys in our neighborhood. My father wanted some too.

By this time I had a new little brother and sister and the sitter was watching us. I was only four but I distinctly remember my father coming home and forcing her into our bedroom, which as I recall was actually a dining room with beds in it and pulling what may have been a curtain over the entrance. I couldn't see what was going on but heard her muffled screams and what seemed to be a struggle and I remember sensing something not being quite right. After a while my father came out all sweaty and disheveled and gave me this burrowing look as if he were trying to gauge what sense I'd made of the whole episode. Once he was satisfied that I was just a dumb kid, he left. Eventually the baby sitter emerged beat-up, slip torn, lip bleeding and crying. I knew something was really funky. Four years old and I knew. Kids are very perceptive, especially ghetto kids because they see a lot of bad things. They know when something has gone wrong, and I knew something was very wrong.

The babysitter left like a wrecked car wobbling away from a traffic accident with us kids standing there in pissy underclothes looking at each other. About twenty minutes later the police came, and after determining pops wasn't there started going through drawers and stuff. My siblings and I were enthralled by their big uniforms with squeaking leather and silver buttons. One of them found a photo and asked, "Is this your daddy?" I said, "Yeah," not realizing I had just fingered my ole man for a nice long stay at the greystone hotel. I would later learn to act dumb in response to any police questioning. Then as suddenly as they had come, they left and there we were, three little kids alone in a cold southside dump. There were no children's services in 1960, and if there had been, I don't think the police would have cared. They were looking for a black man to put in jail . . . high priority. I would later learn that my father was one of a tight group of five that had hung out and grown up together in Atlanta, Georgia. They were good boys. My father for one had grown up in the church. He never could explain to me how they all wound up the way they did, but I did know that he, Ellis, and Clickie turned out to be hopeless drunks, and that another had been killed in the military. I always wondered what became of that fifth kid?

THE JECTS

The projects were cool. There were a lot of kids there, and girls. I really liked girls. When we lived in the tenement there was a girl in our building named Shirley Reye who I used to do nasty stuff with. We'd go under the back stairs, pull our pants down, and grind each other's genitals until they were sore. Once I ground so hard that my dick string broke and started to bleed. We didn't know anything about there being a hole that I could stick my ding-a-ling into, we just knew you had to pull your clothes down and put your stuff together. A little more instruction and I would've been getting flava' at five years old. As it turned out I didn't get my first real piece until I was sixteen, but I played a whole lot of house and doctor on the way because the projects were full of fast girls.

The buildings were huge with hundreds of families living on each city block. Ninety percent of the families were on welfare, "aid" my mother called it, so you can imagine the abundance of little kids running around. It was awesome! We moved into a second floor apartment at 3815 Vernon. There were four kinds of buildings in the 20-block sprawl of projects we lived in. There were the sixteen story Darrow Homes across the park and the six story Extensions up on thirty-seventh street by Doolittle school, then there were some projects between the Darrow Homes and our buildings that were single-family set-ups with upstairs and downstairs. I guess those were for big families. Then there were our projects. You know those big boxes of strike anywhere stick matches with the blue tip? Well, if you sat one of those boxes on its striking side, you'd have a mini replica of my building. One side would be the front of the building, and the other would be the back. Now imagine about twenty of those matchboxes lined up one behind the other and you've got the Ida B. Wells housing project. Each building had five separate entrances with eight apartments in each entrance.

There would generally be a swing or a slide or some monkey bars between the buildings, but some had nothing. There was a wide grass median down the middle of each "front yard" with chains around it to keep kids from riding their bikes on it. There were trees around the buildings and a big park that separated our projects from the Darrow Homes. We referred to everything on the other side of Madden Park as being "across the park." There was a big swimming pool in the middle of the park and in the wintertime the housing authority sprayed water all over the baseball field and made a gigantic ice rink. It was so cool!

IN THE BEGINNING

The school all the kids went to was called Doolittle.

I used to make fun of the school's name saying that they 'did little' and most of the kids I knew did little to challenge that notion. Those kids were dumb as hell. Just think about it, an old beat up grammar school in the middle of a depressed ass housing project. The name fit perfectly. Those poor white teachers were scared as hell of those black kids. They weren't trying to teach them squat, they just wanted to get to the bell to get the hell outta there.

Right away my mother said, "Hell no, you ain't going to no damn Doolittle!"

"Aw momma," I said, "all my friends go there!"

"I don't give a damn, you ain't going to no damn Doolittle!"

Instead she sent me to Mayo Elementary, named after them doctors in Minnesota. My Grandfather lived across the street from the school so she lied and said I lived there too. I don't think she knew, and neither did I, that Mayo was smack dab in the middle of Del Viking territory. You see, every neighborhood in Chicago was divided by gang territories. The whites as well as blacks had their distinct divisions. You couldn't go into the Pollock neighborhood or you'd get killed, and if you were caught around White Sox Park after a game, the Irish Dagos would maim your ass in broad daylight. Likewise, every few blocks in the black neighborhood had a different gang. Everything across the park was Valiant Lords territory and on our side were the Supreme Lords. On the western border of the projects was South Parkway, which would later become Martin Luther King Jr. Drive. Every thing across that street was Del Viking Territory and I had to negotiate it for the next eight years. Kindergarten through sixth grade wasn't really a problem because I was an unassuming little kid and the gang boys didn't mess with me, plus those grades got out fifteen minutes before the bigger kids and I was able to run across South Parkway before they hit the streets. I was real smart in school and I remember most of my teachers. In Kindergarten there was Miss Griffith. I used to look under her dress. She'd play the piano, and when she finished she'd whip her legs out from underneath. Seating was critical. I had to be strategically positioned at her upper left to catch that shot when she swung out. I didn't know much about poon tang, but I definitely knew what panties were. First grade I don't remember, and in second Grade Mrs. Parker was an old bat. My third grade teacher was Mrs. M.C. Johnson. Now she was fine! She had a nice body, hair on her legs, and smelled really good. I asked questions everyday to get her sweet smell over me. In fourth grade there was Mrs. Hudson, and in fifth grade I had Mrs. Harris the big moose. My sixth grade teacher was Ms. B. Johnson. She looked like a black Elizabeth Taylor; necklace, bangles, elaborate hairstyle, make-up, perfume, the whole bit. She was older than a lot of the phillys so she had to be a little hotter and she was. Funny thing though, she never quite got my dander up. I guess it was because I along with everybody else in the school knew the gym teacher Mr. Jamison was killing that. They'd eat lunch together in the gym, and he was the only gym teacher so there were no interruptions. She'd come back after lunch all flushed and her clothes always seemed ruffled where they hadn't been ruffled before. Like I said I was smart. After sixth grade things got crucial. I started getting out of school at three-fifteen with the big kids. I was tall and skinny and the Del Vikings were crawling all over the place. The first day of seventh grade they were on me real tough. When I got to the corner of the schoolyard there was a gang of 'em right there, and as I walked through I kinda got shoved around a little bit. They were all wearing green bandanas and I was scared to death. I could see South Parkway but it was two long blocks away and I didn't know how I was gonna make it.

One of them snatched my book bag out of my hand and as it hit the pavement some candy I had spilled out. That diverted their attention for a split second and that's all it took for me to break out like my ass was on fire. About a half block up the street their fastest runner caught me. He started punching me in the back of the head as he grabbed hold of the back of my jacket. As he snatched at my collar and put on brakes to try and drag me down, I relaxed both arms behind me and shook out of that jacket without missing a beat. As he had shifted his body weight to pull me down and came away with nothing, he tumbled to the ground. I hit a gear I never knew I had, it's called the "running for your life high gear." Those punks never stood a chance. They were in the "running to beat-up somebody gear" and believe me, the two are not synonymous.

The next day I joined the patrol boys. They're like student crossing guards who get to wear a patrol belt, but more importantly, they got out of class ten minutes early to get to their posts. That post never saw my black ass. Once I hit the schoolyard I went immediately into the "running for your life high gear" and didn't cool my jets until I was across South Parkway. You see, my rationale for running all the way home was that even if they spotted me I was already in motion with a head of steam. I told you, I was smart. That went real smoothly until the Captain of the patrol boys Jason Johnson, who everybody called J.J., came to my class and asked my teacher if he could talk with me. I knew something bad was up, but I wasn't going down without a fight.

"I don't know if you know it," he said, "but I'm on your post with you."

"Naw, I didn't know that man," I said trying not to act like I was scared.

"Hell naw you don't know cause you're never there," he said getting in my face.

"Look man," I said not batting an eye, "I live across South Parkway. The Del Vikings have already beat me up once, so I joined the patrol boys so I could get out early and go home before they got out."

"I know," he said. Right then I figured him to be a Del Viking and the jig was up. But he surprised me.

"I can make it so you can keep going home and Mr. Jamison won't know a thing, but it's gon cost you."

"Are you a Del Viking," I asked.

"Hell naw," he asserted.

"How do I know?" I replied.

"You don't," he says. "But you do know I'm the Captain of the patrol boys and if you don't want to deal with me maybe you'd like to talk to Mr. Jamison."

Shit I thought, and he was a little punk too. A little sallow, asthmatic looking nerd. All he needed was glasses and a pocket protector.

"I'm listening," I said, thinking of how I could smack this little punk into the middle of next week and meet him on Thursday.

"A dollar a day, everyday," he demanded. I was stoic.

Finally I was able to speak. "My mother is on welfare, I don't even get lunch money, I get free lunch."

He peered at me with a look of incredulity. "You don't get any money?"

"Nope," I said with an air of helpless finality.

"Well, give me your lunch ticket," he said triumphantly.

"Cool." I reached into my pocket. Every Monday we got our lunch tickets for the week; five tickets connected by perforations like postage stamps. Before I handed them over I made it clear, "If I give you these every week that don't just mean you're not going to tell, it means you'll cover for me all the way right?"

"Yeah, but you've got to still come to patrol meetings and stuff."

"Right, right, but don't look for me on that post."

"I won't," he said. "Every Monday I'll come to your gym class and you give up the tickets."

"All right," I said and we shook hands. That was the first time I'd ever shaken hands on a deal. It felt good.

FIVE BLACK MALES

You know how a group of kids that live on the same block invariably hang out together? Well, that's kinda how the JTs evolved. We were called the JTs because JT, the oldest of the group could whip the other four so he was the natural leader. It's funny how that theory was never tested. We all just sorta fell in line and that was that. One day JT's brother Ray said, "I can't believe ya'll following this little punk," pointing at JT. "You know what, I'm gonna start callin' ya'll the JT's, those are his initials you know." It stuck. There was JT, Woodrow, Duh Duh, Dino, and me, Lamont, Mont for short. I can't remember exactly when we started hanging out, but I specifically remember the day the Del Vikings chased me home. My boys were all hanging out on the grassy median on our side of South Parkway laughing their asses off. JT of course spoke first.

"Damn, they were on you man!" I gave him the finger with my hands on my knees and my head bowed trying to catch my breath.

"You looked just like a little fag running across that street, go back and do it again Lamont," howled Woodrow nearly doubled over in laughter.

"I don't see why you go to that punk-ass school anyway, you's a goof-ball" added Duh Duh, "I'd tell my momma to kiss my ass if she tried to make me go there." They all thought that was really funny and proceeded to fall off their bikes cracking up. When I'd finally caught my breath enough to talk I told them, "You punks could've thrown some bottles or something."

"Shidd, knowin you, you probably would've run right into one," Dino chimed in. Then I noticed they were all on their bikes in their play clothes and I'd just run straight home from school.

"Why is that ya'll always out playin way before I get home?"

"Man those scary crackers let us walk out whenever we get ready," said Woodrow.

"Then he just come git me," added JT

"You know it," agreed Duh Duh.

I was disgusted with Duh-Duh and showed it. "Yo B-19 ass need to stay in school as much as you can." They all laid out again cracking up. B-19 is a basement classroom at Doolittle (thus the B designation) where they house the Exceptional Education students. Duh Duh never liked it when anybody brought it up.

"Yo momma sit next to me bitch," he barked hurtfully.

"You ain't even got a momma you foster freak." I had to get him back.

"At least my momma don't suck dick," he countered.

"If my momma did suck dick she'd never be as good as yo big lipted ass." I'd regained all of my faculties.

"Leave him alone Mont, he can't help it if you run like a lil' bitch," interrupted JT while me and Duh Duh gave each other playful looks of disgust. It was true, they could leave school whenever they wanted and nobody stopped them, no hall monitors, no security, nobody. The place was like a zoo. Damn I wished I could go there. You know, a lot of people think that just because you live in the projects you're an uneducated thief who's busted, disgusted, and can't be trusted, but that's the farthest thing from the truth. The kids in the projects were just like any others; fun loving, happy, and innocent. There were one or two bad boys on every block, but those were older boys who were in the gang. Even then not too many of them had guns. That would come later. The point needs to be made that we were all good boys from decent families. We wore neat, clean clothes, went to school (for the most part), didn't smoke, cursed because it sounded cool not because we used that kind of language in our homes, and generally had every opportunity to become productive members of society. There are those quick to tell you white America has "life-mines" scattered all around specifically to blow young black males off the prosperity map. There are those to tell you that the system has been massaged and cultivated over the decades to pull the football out from under all the black Charley Browns until they quit the game in frustration and ventured over to the dark side where all the life-mines really were. I guess the ones who make it to college have certainly beat the odds, but still face the established hurdles of culturally biased standardized tests, white professors, and the all mighty good ole' boy network. They say that if you can make it through all of that you're good... but not all will make it.

3757 SOUTH GILES AVENUE

One of the reasons going to Mayo Elementary wasn't so bad was that my grandfather lived across the street from the school. I loved my grandfather to the point of idolization. He was strong, wise, good looking, and could fix anything on earth. He was the patriarch of the family, which took on increased importance to me because I didn't have a daddy. I'd sneak over to his house everyday for lunch (since I had no lunch tickets) and my grandmother would serve the best food in the world. Having them there made up for everything that could have possibly been missing in my life. The bare places in the cupboard where the welfare food allotment failed us were filled by my grandmother's gourmet fried chicken and sweet spaghetti, and the ostensible positive black male role model who was in jail was never missed. My grandfather made up for that twenty times over. Although he was uneducated he talked to me about life and I gobbled up his wisdom greedily. He owned his own building with several tenants and kept it up superbly. He let me help shovel coal into the stoker, hold fence-posts he was cementing in place, and knead the putty when he installed new windows. Experiences like this for little boys, black or white, with men are so important it defies qualification. Little boys don't learn how to be men from big mama, they don't develop self-confidence and awareness of themselves by sitting around listening to women talk. They don't become good students, proactive helpers, and potentially strong leaders by themselves, they get these things from responsible men who care. I had that in my Grandfather. He wasn't an old, feeble Grandfather either. He was a strong, robust, tower of a man with huge hands and a no-nonsense approach to everything. I remember once stopping by before school and finding him knocking down a bedroom wall to enlarge the living room.

"Granddaddy can I stay and help you? You probably need a hand cleaning up all this plaster and stuff, and guess what? You didn't even cover the couches, they're getting dust all over them. I'm gon' run in the back and get some old sheets from Grandmamma and take care of that." That day turned out to be a galvanizing moment in my life, working side by side with my grandfather as a man . . . handing him the right tools even before he asked for them, learning how to sweep (which was harder than I imagined), and then sitting down to eat after a job well done with our iced tea in large Mason jars. I adored that man.

I later understood that those were the kinds of days every young boy needs in order to know he has worth, to encode a particular confidence to be unwittingly transcribed at a later date of anxious destiny.

That two story brownstone at 3757 South Giles Avenue transcended the wind stopping power of brick and mortar . . . it stopped a whole lot of other stuff . . . invisible stuff.

J.T.

JT was a natural leader who took charge of everything because he was older than the rest of us by about a year. He was also the first one of us to get some poon-tang (cause he had a girlfriend and we didn't), and I already mentioned he could whip all of us. That's generally the way it was with any crowd, the one who could beat all the others made the rules. He was a short powerfully built dude who walked kinda pigeon toed. His real name was Jerome Tate, but for some reason he didn't like Jerome and only his mother called him that. Sometimes when we wanted to annoy him we'd call him by his real name, but that usually resulted in somebody getting shoved up against a brick wall, hard, so we just called him JT. He lived on the first floor in the yard behind mine with his mother and two brothers. His mother was even shorter than him, a compacted, fine little thing. I always wanted to look under her dress. Seems like that plump juicy ass of hers would make her house dress rise right up. Unfortunately, with JT around I couldn't get many good looks. JT's older brother went to Vietnam and came back a dope fiend. His younger brother had a white daddy and we constantly teased JT and him about it to the point that JT didn't want him hanging around us too much. My mother called him a trick baby; I called him disco mix. He was a goofy little dude who liked snakes and insects and stuff and was always studying them. He irritated the hell out of JT.

Sometimes he'd turn the corner carrying a jar full of grass wearing some plastic camera around his neck and JT would beat the shit out of him for being such a Geek. We'd laugh till we couldn't breathe. We came to realize JT kinda had a chip on his shoulder. Maybe because he didn't have a daddy, but mostly because he was short. He had a little man complex like you wouldn't believe. He had to be the best at everything: baseball, football, softball, swimming, whatever. He felt so proud to have a girlfriend and getting poon-tang it was sickening. He had a fine girlfriend too, Betty Jefferson. Man she was smokin. We used to try and figure out how he got her. She was taller than him and could've had any dude in the jects yet she chose JT; granted he was a nice guy. He was clean cut, smart, athletic, a natural leader, and he didn't go around blabbing his mouth about what they did behind closed doors. I remember one time I asked him, "JT, you tearing that ass up ain't you?" He gave me this Hollywood look like Tyrone Power and said, "Man I'm a pee-yump, (pimp for the hip impaired) what you think?"

"Where ya'll be doin it at?" I asked.

"We go to my house, where you think?"

Since I'd gotten him this far I couldn't resist, "She suck yo dick?"

He gave me this look like, 'nigga please,' "you need some flava in yo life boy so you can have some memories."

Now what was that supposed to mean? I guess that's why he was so cool, he could play you off by making you think. JT was a Capricorn like Muhammad Ali and Richard Nixon, "Born leaders" as he put it. He went to Doolittle but he wasn't dumb, he was gonna pass and probably go to Wendell Phillips, the neighborhood high school. By all indications JT would be the first to taste success, the first to move out of the projects, and the one to show us all how it should be done.

WOODROW

Woodrow had it all because his father ran the dope house. His real name was Charles Woods, but JT started calling him Woodrow and of course everybody started calling him that too. He lived in the yard behind JT's on the third floor. Although JT was the leader of our little group, he would never get too harsh with Woody because he had two big brothers who were bona fide gangsters, not to mention his kingpin father who everybody called Papa D. Now to understand Woodrow's place in the hood one has to understand the climate of the times, and the reverence with which the dope man is endowed in the black community. In 1968 heroine was king. We're talking Jimmy Hendrix, the emergence of flower power, the Black Panther movement and Superfly. In a segment of society that was unable, or not allowed to move freely in the American commerce system, the dope man wore many hats. To all thieves and hustlers he was the local fence who bought hot items at one-third the store price (they called it "dope fiend" prices). To many parents who couldn't make ends meet he was the local bank who would loan money at no interest (as long as you brought the money back when you said you would). If a kid wanted to set up a car washing business, a lemonade stand, a sewing business or whatever, Papa D would loan you the money and you just paid him back when you made your profits. If someone in your family was a regular customer you always got a turkey at Christmas and your kids never went without presents under the tree. He was a kind benefactor to the entire neighborhood, the black man's financial institution loved by everyone and protected at all costs. Looking back I realize that's how he proliferated all those years without so much as a scratch. First and foremost however, he was the pusher man, doctor feel-good, your Friday night friend open twenty four-seven three sixty-five. Now you understand who Woody was. He was the young prince. My mother called him a spoiled brat but he wasn't. That was what was so special about him, he was regular. There were no designer clothes out then so he wasn't jumping clean. He was just a kid so he didn't have a car, although he was the first to have a banana seat five-speed Schwinn fastback bicycle. But even then I had a pimp Sears bike with a light on it and saddlebags so what's the big deal? He was just one of the fellas, cool as hell, but like I said he had brothers JoJo and Bruno, and they were different. They were straight leg breakers, big, bad dudes who would scare you stiff just looking at you. Once you got into the family you kinda got the flavor of what was really going on. Papa D always had a very sexy young girl as his protege, many times white. I always figured he was bonin' them. Woodrow's mother was a nurse. Papa D called her "Butch" (it took many years before I figured that one out, duh). She did back room abortions and her medical expertise later helped them branch out into prescription drugs like syrup and Ritalin. Now Woodrow also had a big sister named Darlene who was as fine as coke and ain't no joke. The girl was thicker than cornbread. She went to Phillips and could sing like a Canary. She was smart, beautiful, motivated, and untouched by all the street level shit going on around her as was Woodrow. The family was really nice. If the two brothers weren't around and you were to visit, you'd never be the wiser. They didn't drive Cadillacs or wear fancy clothes and they didn't have a fabulously decorated crib or anything like that. They were just about like everyone else except they had a large supply of disposable cash. And when I say cash I mean just that: dirty, crumpled up $5's, $10's and $20's, hundreds of them with seemingly no end. Their business was handled by "soldiers" they had all over the neighborhood. After I became wise I began to notice an inconspicuous young gentleman downstairs who caught all the traffic at the house. Then I later found out there was another on thirty-ninth, thirty-eighth, thirty-seventh, and thirty-fifth streets. They had their thing together. From these placid surroundings one could visualize this going on forever. Like I said they were widely loved, Woodrow was a princely lad, and everything was skippy dippy.

DINO

Dino was a beautiful athletic specimen. He was as fluid on a field as any superstar you could think of. He had catlike reflexes, the eye of a hawk, the hands of a surgeon, and a heart made of cast iron steel. There's generally a plethora of gifted athletes in any black neighborhood, but this boy was truly special. He dominated every game he played be it with guys our age, big boys, or grown men, no one could stop him, everyone idolized him, and the girls simply adored him. The killer part was, he hung with us. We got much flava when we were with Dino. If we were hustling up some cash for something we'd always get Dino to ask for it because nobody ever said no to him. If we were trying to get in a party, a picnic, or even the Y.W.C.A., we'd push Dino right up front and BLAM! like magic we were in. His rep was so large girls would let us do things to them in hopes that Dino would be jumping in somewhere along the line. The boy had all state, all American, all Heisman million dollar bonus baby written all over him. The only thing was, he didn't give a damn about school.

Every day when I shot across South Parkway he was there dribbling a ball.   "Dino, where's the fellas?"

"They ain't got out yet," he'd say dribbling through his legs, spinning the ball, and all kinds of cool stuff.

"Well what are you doin' out?"

"I was sick today."

"Yeah right," I'd say while making a lunge for the ball thinking I had his attention diverted. He'd effortlessly swing the ball around his back and through his legs as I went hurtling face first into the crete (concrete for the hip-impaired).

"Boy don't be no fool, come on try to take the ball." Now my first instinct would be to say, "nigga I ain't scrapin' up my knees messin' with you." But I realize he's been outside dribbling all day hoping for someone to come along to sharpen his chops on, and besides, he's our meal ticket, gotta keep him happy. So I strip off my jacket as I give him a lean, hungry look. "Prepare to get picked clean punk."

"Oh hell yeah," he'd say smiling as he dribbles the ball real low to the ground never taking his eyes off me. "You take this ball and I'll give you everything I've got in my pocket." He shouldn't have said that because I didn't have a thing in my pockets, not even a lunch ticket. I lunge in to the left, he moves the ball. I dive to the right, he moves the ball. I grab him around the waist with both hands and he's still dribbling behind his back!

"Hell naw dammit you cheatin'," I cry in frustration.

"How am I cheatin', you all but tackling me wit yo goofy ass," he retorts laughing hard, but still not out of control enough for me to get the ball.

"You gotta show the ball," I whine.

"See," he says putting the ball right at my nose. Of course I snatch at it but it's not there any more. With my hands on my knees gasping for air I come the only way I can. "Yo dumb ass ain't gon get on no team if you don't go to school."

"I'm going to school tomorrow, I told you I was sick today," he offers while feinting at me, proffering a chance to try at the ball. All I can do is shake my head because I'm too tired to argue.

Dino was from the biggest family of the group. He had three brothers and two sisters and his mother kept them neat as hell. I mean starched neat. In every black neighborhood there's a family with no daddy, on welfare, no car, but as neat and clean as the board of health. I had never been in Dino's house, nor had anyone else, but whenever any one of those kids stepped outside to play you best believe their khakis were starched, their gym shoes had been in the washing machine, their tee shirts were sparkling fresh, their hair was combed to perfection, and their faces were greased. Everybody used Vaseline on their faces to knock the ash off. I'm sure there was lotion available but black folks couldn't see the sense in buying lotion with only one use. You could use Vaseline as skin lotion, first aid gel and hair grease. Additionally, you could buy a whole tub of it for only a couple dollars. Vaseline was a staple in every home. They were polite kids too. "Yes ma'am, no ma'am," and the only time they cursed was when there were no adults around. When they came home from school they came up out of those school clothes and put on their crisp play clothes. Funny thing though, I never saw Dino with any books, only a ball. As we got older Dino would talk about his mother's boyfriend being a detective, but we never saw him.

DUH DUH

Duh Duh's life was strange from the beginning. He didn't live with his mother or father. In fact, in all the years I knew Duh Duh, whose real name was Raymond Bluitt, neither he nor anyone else ever mentioned his parents. He lived with his aunt, who for the life of me I can't remember ever seeing. I kinda remember going to his crib once and it was so freaky I never went back. Maybe I blocked out the memory of his aunt because it was so weird. He lived in JT's yard on the third floor of a clean hallway that was always locked. You see, every entrance door at one time had a lock to which the occupants of every apartment had a key. Some hallways were always locked, like the ones where old folks lived. Most of the hallways, like mine, were never locked, never had a lock there in the first place, just a hole. Anyway, Duh Duh's aunt was real old and his crib had that funky old-folks smell. They had that old heavy antique lookin furniture with doilies on the backs of everything. The big trip though was that they had no television, no radio, and no lights. None. In the projects every room had a fixture on the wall into which you screwed a light bulb. Well, they didn't have one light bulb in their whole place, not one lamp, not even a clock or a radio with a light on it. At high noon the windows were up and there was light, but at night there was complete darkness. The weight of this situation affected Duh Duh too. Sometimes when we talked about family or toys or things that went on in our homes, a pall would fall over the group because Duh Duh was awkwardly left out. It was kinda pitiful. Anytime during the day if you wanted Duh Duh you had to go around to the back of his building and call up to his window that was always open. Even in the wintertime his window was open. At night he was always out no matter how cold or how late, he would be out. For some reason he chose my building to hang out in. I don't know how many times I've come out of my crib and went downstairs and he'd be down there rockin. Just sittin on the steps rockin back and forth. Sometimes when me and my brother and sister are in the crib arguing about something and I needed the testimony of someone who was there, I'd simply go to the door, open it, and yell.

"Duh Duh," and sho as shit he'd answer.

"Yo."

"Come here man." You'd hear Duh Duh eagerly bound up the stairs.

"What up?"

"Man tell them that Ervin chased us all the way to thirty-fifth street." Duh Duh fell out laughing. He laughed so hard my little brother got impatient.

"Well what happened nigga, damn!"

Duh Duh clutching his heart and between pants said, "Aw man that fool had us goin boy, he just wouldn't give up, he wanted our asses."

My sister figuring me and Duh Duh had already been in the hall getting our story together, tried to slip him up cause she knew he was slow.

"What time was this?" She knew Ervin was never out past dusk, not even into dusk. Hell, three, four o'clock Ervin was locked down.

"Maybe two, two thirty, then once we took off from Alco's he disappeared." Alco's was an all night drug store on thirty-fifth street. My sister didn't want to believe it though because Ervin had never been on thirty-fifth street in his life. Hell, Ervin had never been across South Parkway; you see, Ervin was retarded.

A DIFFERENT DRUMMER

Once I got past the Del Vikings and realized it was a good thing my boys didn't go to my school, I found out that I really liked school. In fact, I loved it. Learning stuff was really exciting to me and I especially liked field trips. Back in Chicago at that time you had to pay to go on field trips. Like when we went to Springfield Illinois, Abraham Lincoln's hometown (I think I read somewhere he wasn't really born there) and the State Capitol. The teacher gave me a letter to take home asking for twelve dollars to pay for it. I remember running across South Parkway and stopping to read it and my eyes filled with tears because I knew my mother didn't have twelve dollars to give me. She was in the kitchen making spaghetti with meat in it, my favorite.

"What's this?"

"It's for a field trip to Springfield, the Land of Lincoln." I stood there wide-eyed not showing any emotion one way or the other. I'd always gone on all the other field trips with my classes because they were all $1.50 per kid or something like that, but this was the biggest amount ever and I knew going in I'd be sitting in Mrs. Brown's class with all the other bummy kids whose parents couldn't afford to send them.

"Do you want to go?" she asked looking down at me with her eyes so full of love and what seemed to be an excessive amount of moisture.

"Yeah momma I do."

"Okay," she said with resolution. "Give momma a hug." I leapt onto her neck like a baby possum clinging during a high climb. And there were tears ... I saw 'em. I didn't really understand; all I knew was I was going to Springfield! I ran outta that apartment and played baseball like Ernie Banks, Billy Williams and Ferguson Jenkins all wrapped in one! I never missed a field trip. I went to every museum, play, zoo, you name it I was there. I was in every science fair no matter how much the supplies cost. I had a potato that lit up a light bulb one year and two telephones hooked up together for another. Then in fifth grade my mother made the most profound move of my educational life: she got me a subscription to Reader's Digest. Oh ... My ... God. That thing was jam packed with beautiful fictional stories, educational articles, humor, and the single most valuable component of my WHOLE ENTIRE LIFE, **It Pays To Increase Your Word power.** I devoured them. I knew the day they'd be delivered every other week and I'd pounce on the mailman's ass like he was a pork chop. My front yard was always full of activity: kids playing ball, hide and seek, girls jumpin' rope, boys shooting marbles, fellas hanging out and I'd be in my bedroom dancing through that Reader's Digest like Tiny Tim through tulips. I wouldn't read it all at one time though, no, got to make it last for two weeks.

I also remember when I was in fifth grade the Big Moose gave me a letter to take home to my mother. It wasn't stapled so as soon as I ran across South Parkway I read it. They wanted her to come to the school to discuss my 'academic placement.' I knew academic had to do with school and education stuff. Were they trying to put me out or something? The meeting was in Mr. Walker's office, the Assistant Principal who never smiled. He'd paddled me once in there and believe me once was enough. So needless to say I was a little worried. I didn't know if I was getting kicked out or kicked in the butt. Either way it was terrible. He asked my mother to come in first and they'd call me in later. So I sat in the outer office with Mrs. Randall his secretary. She had more hair than anyone I'd ever seen in my life! It was like a ten foot tall Tastee Freeze ice cream cone that didn't melt, move, or anything. It just sat there and hypnotized you if you looked at it too long. I could hear my mother and Mr. Walker's voices inside his office because my chair was right by the door, but I couldn't really understand what they were saying. I heard Mr. Walker say, "your son" and I heard my mother say, "uh huh," so I leaned in towards the door as far as I could without Mrs. Randall saying something and concentrated really hard on tuning her typewriter out so I could hear some more words. Just then she pushed her chair out from the desk and I knew I was dead. Mr. Walker was gonna paddle me, my mother was gon' whoop me, and Mrs. Randall was gon' get some too. As she walked around from behind her desk she looked right at me and I tried my best to turn invisible, to just melt right into that chair until I was simply not there anymore.

God saved me though, because she kept walking right past me, out the door and clicketty-clacked her high-heeled shoes right down the hall into the ladies bathroom! I jumped up and plastered my ear into the crack of Mr. Walkers door as I bit my lower lip. " H e tested off the charts," said Mr. Walker. "You should consider sending him to the accelerated school."

Just then I heard the squeak of the ladies room door and Mrs. Randall's high-heels clicketty-clacking back down the hall. I slid back into my chair in a daze over what I thought I'd heard. What did he mean I'd 'tested off the charts?' Did he mean I cheated on a test? Because I didn't! Me, Gregory Case, and Marilyn Fowler had a legitimate grade battle going on since the third grade but we weren't cheating. I was beating them on a daily fair and square, especially in math. They couldn't touch me in long division, fractions, decimals, none of that stuff.

And what was accelerated school? Mr. Walker never called me into his office. Him and my mother came out, he shook her hand, and told Mrs. Randall to give me a hall pass, and to call Ms. Harris and let her know I was on my way back to class. He never smiled, not once. As soon as I got back to my classroom I went straight to the bookshelf and got a dictionary. I knew the accelerator pedal on a car made it go faster, so what . . . he wanted me out faster? **ac.cel.er.ate** – increase in amount or extent.

What? I repeated it to myself a few times. "He tested off the charts and maybe should go to the accelerated school." They weren't trying to kick me out . . . I tested off the charts! My grades were MORE than 100! They wanted to send me to a school to increase the amount of work . What!? Oh hell no, I wanted to stay at Mayo! I like the kids here, I didn't want to go to school with a bunch of nerds!

I eyeballed my mother all that night because as soon as she fixed her mouth to say 'accelerated school' I was gon' go berserk, but she never mentioned it and neither did I. After that I entered oratorical contests, spelling bees, you name it, my teachers put me in it. And if it cost money, my mother made it happen. She'd go up in her brassier, pull out her tattered coin purse, and separate those dollars like they were clinging together for dear life. And you know what? Only once in a while did I annoy my boys with my scholastic prowess. They knew about me, they accepted me . . . and if I got too cocky JT beat me up.

A CAST OF CHARACTERS

Kids are cruel. If you're fat they'll call you a fat ass everyday. If your Momma is a slut, trust me, it wasn't no secret. The projects, teeming with kids of every shape, size, and emotional hue were fertile grounds for colorful nicknames and outwardly embarrassing descriptors that became an accepted way of life. Kids weren't humiliated and either you held your own or you were a sissy, simple as that. Just like in medieval plays where characters' names described their temperament such as: Tibet Talk-A-Pace for a big mouth gossip, Penelope Pinchpenny for a cheapskate, or Harmony Blue Blossom for the wholesome town virgin, we gave kids names that told the whole story.

There was this boy we called The Big Cheese because he had extremely yellow teeth and was fat, black and greasy.

There was Daryll Mangum who had broken his right arm playing outside. While his arm was still in a cast he broke the left arm (he drank a lot of pop). Kids started calling him "Double Broke," then "Double D." Thirty years later everybody would know him as "Dub."

Bone Man and Little Man need no explanations. There was this really tall girl in our neighborhood named Barbara, they called her 6-2 (for 6' 2"). Frog was one of the neighborhood gang boys who looked just like a toad . . . for real.

One-Eyed Jack was in B-19 so we all knew he was kinda dumb. Many summers ago this girl named Niecy threw a rock and hit him in the eye by accident. His eye was all blurry and grey like someone stirring black and white paint together in a can. This made him look really, really stupid. On top of that he was kinda fat, drooled, and spoke in this breathy, labored, slush-mouthed manner that made it seem like he was struggling to breathe. His name wasn't really Jack, it was Harold or something but everybody called him One-Eyed Jack so that was his name.

There was Hippity Hop, Roach, and Fly who you'd think looked like a fly but that wasn't it at all. He was cool, and the movie Super Fly had just come out. He started wearing these big hats, slick sunglasses, and long pimp coats so everybody started calling him Fly. This was made more hilarious because his former nickname was Bo Peep!

I remember this bully kid named Booty Green. He took my mini bike from me one time and my Mother had to go across the park and take it back. I don't know why they called him Booty Green and I don't want to know. There was Papa Hard and Big Money which I don't understand at all because Big Money didn't even have a car as I remember. Odd Rob walked funny and of course everybody knew Duh Duh who was as dumb as a box of hammers. He'd get mad if you talked about him being in B-19, but answered to Duh Duh his whole life . . . go figure

WE HAD SO MUCH FUN

I have to tell you about the time Ervin chased us to thirty-fifth street. He lived in the building across from mine on the third floor. He was a grown man of maybe thirty something with the mind of a ten year old. He kept this old baseball glove with him everywhere he went and was always ready to play. He wasn't good, but sometimes when we needed an extra player we'd pick Ervin. He was always an easy out at bat because his reaction was slow. So if you had Ervin on your side your team always got to bat first. He was a little better in the field though because he'd stop the ball. You could hit a scorcher right at him that a normal kid would jump out of the way of, but Ervin would step right in front of it and try to catch it. He rarely made a sparkling play in the field, but he would stop the ball. Another quick kid would run over, grab the ball, and throw the guy out. Ervin would still be looking around for the ball. Sometimes we'd tease him by calling him stupid and running. One day we were sitting around drinking pop after playing ball.

"Look at Ervin's retarded ass, walking around with his booty all humped up, hey Ervin, you stupid mutha fucka!" Dino said.

Ervin stopped his little quickstep hippity-hop walk and cocked his head to one side as if to say, you talkin' to me?

"You shouldn't make retarded people mad, they'll snap on your ass," Duh Duh said.   Just then Ervin began lumbering towards us lookin' crazier than we'd ever seen him look.

"Oh shit," JT said, as he jumped up and started running. Needless to say, we all jumped up and ran like hell. We ran between the buildings all the way to the other end near South Parkway and stopped by a fence that allowed us to see anybody coming from both directions.

Woodrow said, "Damn Dino, why you fuckin' with Ervin man, you know he strong!"
"Don't worry man, he can't run fast," replied Dino.

"He ain't gotta run fast to catch Duh Duh," I added flipping my pop-top at Duh Duh.

"Fuck you Mont, he'd break yo little skinny ass."

"Yo auntie," I snapped back. We were having a swell time almost forgetting we had somebody on our tail when out of nowhere up popped Ervin big as hell right next to Woodrow.

"Who ovah heah called me stupid?"
YIKES! We must have shot up in the air a hundred feet before our feet started working.

"Arghhhh," we screamed as we dropped those pops and ran for dear life. He had scared the shit out of us! We didn't know where we were going, but nobody was slowing down either. I looked back and saw Ervin clodding along behind us in the way one of those horror movie monsters do, just steadily walking while the poor victim runs his ass off.

"He's coming," I screamed. We hit the running for your life high gear and didn't stop till we were on thirty-fifth street.

"All right stop man stop, you know good and damn well Ervin ain't coming to no thirty-fifth street," ordered JT.

"Damn Dino," barked Duh Duh, who was coughing, spitting, and gagging.

"I didn't know that fool was gon' chase us all day," spat Dino, hardly breathing hard. Just then I noticed a man standing on the opposite corner in front of the Supreme Life Insurance building that looked a lot like Ervin.

"Look, is that Ervin," I asked incredulously.

"Hell naw," assured JT. "How in the hell could he have gotten up here that fast, and besides, you know good and goddamn well you ain't gon' see Ervin on thirty fifth street."

Still, all our eyes were glued on that figure. When the light changed he started walking toward us and it didn't take long to recognize the quickstep, hippity hop walk. Our eyes widened, we clutched each other's clothing, and as he broke into a little lumbering trot our hair stood straight up.

"Oh shit," we all screamed at the same time. It seemed all five of us wanted to go in a different direction. I wanted to go South, Dino wanted to go North, Woodrow wanted to go East, and Duh Duh, who always follows JT was going West with him. We ran smack into each other like the five stooges.

"This way," shouted Dino.

No, this way," ordered JT.

"Hell naw," screamed Woodrow, that's the way home, we want to run farther away, maybe he'll stop!"

"Come on goddamit," I cried. Just then, as if by Hollywood magic, he was on us,   "Who ovah heah called me stupid?" I know it seems impossible to be laughing so hard your side hurts and at the same time experiencing the most horrific moment of your life, but that's what was happening. It was so ludicrous because here we were running in terror from what was in essence a ten-year-old kid, yet the shit was serious because nobody knew what his crazy ass would do. And he had to be mad, snapped, or something cause he had chased us to thirty-fifth! We tripped all over ourselves in hilarity, exhaustion, and straight up fear for the next five blocks. At one point I grabbed Duh Duh and tried to drag him to a stop.

"Here he is Ervin," I shouted, playing like I was going to hold him until Ervin caught up. Duh Duh had a fit.

"Let me go mutha fucka, let me go!" He had some of the truest fear in his eyes you'd ever want to see, and we all nearly died laughing. Which, had we known then, would have been our preference. You see, Ervin wasn't all that followed us. With hooded robe and sharpened scythe wrapped in seemingly innocuous events, the pale rider would eventually catch us.

In the meantime, we didn't go back to my yard because we didn't know where Ervin was so we decided to go roof climbing.

ROOF CLIMBING

Roof climbing was an art. You had to be nimble, daring, and most of all an adventurer. With roof climbing you never knew where you'd wind up. There were a few roofs that were our favorites. We liked to climb B. Heller's roof because nobody had ever gotten into their building and there was always the chance we'd be the first. B. Heller's was a spice manufacturing company and we'd always sneeze like crazy whenever we climbed their roof. It was a sprawling warehouse complex with all the buildings connected, so once you got on top of the first roof, you could explore all the others. You never knew what you would find on the top of a roof. There were of course your every day items like old gym shoes, bicycle tires, and pop bottles, but occasionally you'd find something that wasn't supposed to be there like a brand new baseball glove, or some cool ass sunglasses. Something that someone may have thrown up there in anger that the owner couldn't retrieve. Once I found a knife, a big one in the sheath and everything. JT tried to trick me out of it.

"Damn," he said wide-eyed, "my knife!"

I gave him a 'nigga please' look. "What choo mean yo knife?"

"I lost that up here when me and Earl Stingly came up here."

Woodrow and Dino looked back and forth between me and JT with little crooked smiles on their faces, waiting to dog me out if I gave up the knife.

"You must be crazy," I defended, "you think you getting this knife you best be pullin' out some money."

"O.K. just let me see it," he finally confessed.

"Hell naw, you might try to run with it."

"Where the hell am I gonna run, we're on a damn roof," replied JT.

"I'll hold it," I warned. "Just look, don't touch."

Shit like that happened all the time. That's why once we got on a roof, everybody wanted to be out front. The person who climbed up before you was supposed to stay and give you a hand up, but most of the time they took off running in hopes of being the big Marco Polo of the group discovering something good. We usually looked for a fence that was close to the wall that we could climb, or a tree that hung over the roof that we could drop down from. Sometimes we had to scale the front facade of buildings in order to get on the roof, or go to the top floor of buildings and climb through the roof access hatch in the ceiling. We were good. Once though, I remember we messed up. Across South Parkway there were tenement buildings. They went from thirty-ninth to thirty-eighth street. Once you got on the first one you could go all the way to the end of the block over the different roofs. Well, this one roof was higher than the one next to it so we had to hang and drop to the house below. We shouldn't have done that because when we got to the end of the row of houses, looked over, threw stuff on people down on the street and generally had a good time, we realized we couldn't get down.

"Damn Lamont," Woodrow exclaimed, "yo dumb ass got us stuck."

"I got us stuck, how did I get us stuck?"

"You the one that kept saying we could hang and jump, now what we gon do?"   "Wait a minute," Dino said, "maybe we can go down a back porch."

So we started looking over the back edges of the roofs.

"Oh man, look at that big ass dog," said Duh Duh's scary ass. Sure enough though, there was a big, nasty looking German Shepherd in the yard.

"That's out," said JT, "let's check the one next door."

Wouldn't you know they had a dog too, bigger than the nasty looking one. The one yard without a dog didn't have a back porch, just sheer wall all the way down to the ground.

"Damn, what we gon do now," begged Duh Duh as he looked imploringly at JT the way he always did. JT sat down and put his chin in his hands. We all sat down, put our chins in our hands and looked at JT. He was our leader, now was the time to lead.

"Let's look over every inch of these roofs, don't miss nuthin', there must be a way down," he barked as he hopped to his feet.

"Come on Woodrow let's go this way," I said heading to the North end of the roof. Me and Woodrow always stuck together because we were more like each other. Duh Duh was a retard who didn't have any ideas of his own and mostly followed JT. Dino was kinda quiet and mostly showed his personality through some sort of sport. JT was the oldest and had a girlfriend, so that naturally left me and Woodrow to hang out.

"Well?" shouted JT over five or six roofs. Wood and I just shook our heads.

"What about ya'll," I shouted back.

"Hell naw," said Dino.

"Well that's it," said Woodrow, "I guess were stuck."

The adventure was over and now we were scared.

"How we gittin' down," questioned Duh Duh looking to JT for the answer.

"Shut up," said Woodrow getting frustrated.

"You shut up," snapped Duh Duh. "You don't tell me when to talk."

"Naw, I tell that decrepit ass aunt of yours, old hide-and go-seek ass bitch."

"Man ain't nobody talk about yo old dope fiend ass daddy and yo fat ass momma," Duh Duh cried as he used both hands to push Woodrow in the chest. Just as Woodrow was about to lunge at Duh Duh, JT jumped in the middle.

"Would you two fags shut up, pretty soon it's gon' be dark and ya'll gon' have to sleep with each other."

Woodrow and Duh Duh cut each other dirty looks and snatched away in disgust. "So what we gon do JT?" implored Dino.

"I saw a building down there with a whole bunch of stuff on the front, maybe we can climb down that way."

We went a couple of roofs down and you know how some buildings have a bunch of ornate frescos and gargoyle looking sculptures on the front? Well, that's what this building was like.

"You must be crazy," cried Woodrow, "how we gon' climb down the front of this building?"

"Well stay yo ass up here," said JT as he swung one leg over the ledge planting his foot on a concrete overhang. We were about four stories up and things down on the street looked real little, so nobody was in a hurry to follow JT this time, not even Duh Duh who for once questioned his idol's reasoning.

"Are you sure you've checked everything?"

"Stay there, I'm getting off this roof," answered JT with a smugness that reassured us that this was the right way down. JT could do that, that's why he was the leader. So we all leaned over to see where he was going to put his foot next, then where after that and so on. Many years later I would see rock climbing on the Wide World of Sports that looked just like what we were doing, only they had ropes on them just in case they fell. We had nothing between us but oops, air, and pure concrete.

"Well come on you pussies," hollered JT, maybe three or four feet down the front of the building.

"Go ahead Dino," offered Duh Duh as we all parted like the Red Sea to let Dino pass.

"What choo mean go ahead Dino? You know JT is yo daddy, you follow him," said Dino indignantly.

"Go ahead Dino, you can do it," I said as I grabbed Dino's arm urging him to the edge. Dino snatched away.

"Let me go, I'll go when I'm ready."

As it turned out we all wound up on that building's facade clinging like roaches. Soon we had an audience including the landlord and the police.

"Don't look down," people would yell. Hell, they just made us more afraid. I wish I had a picture; it could have gone in Jet Magazine.

FIRE-LICKED DREAMS

One day not long after the roof climbing episode my mother made me take the garbage out. In fact, she had me doing a whole lotta stuff that day. I cleaned the tub (one of my most hated chores in all the world), mopped the kitchen floor, and worked her toes (you don't want to know). Anyway, attached to the back of every building was an incinerator where everybody tossed their garbage. It looked like a big barbecue grill made of bricks with a super steel door on the front that you opened and let your trash slide down. When there was a fire started down in the basement you could feel a little heat rising when you opened the door.

So I take the garbage down, and sitting next to the incinerator was a medium sized cardboard box filled with paperback books. But they weren't regular books, they had University of Illinois, Michigan State University, De Paul University and stuff like that on the front of them. They were college catalogues! I was immediately fascinated. I'd never seen anything like that before. I'd heard of college but I didn't know anybody who'd gone there and in fact, I had no idea what a college looked like. I guess college was sort of an allegorical vision in my mind without shape and texture.

I sat down (I don't even remember what I did with the garbage), enthralled by the ivy and the smiles on the faces of students wearing thick school sweaters emblazoned with big W's, M's, and U's on them. Some of the catalogues had bell towers on the front of them while others had pictures of huge library rooms with long polished wooden tables adorned with green glass lamps. There were athletic fields, theatre kids, and science labs with students wearing safety goggles. I wanted to do that! On the back of each one it said Brenda Oglesby . . . she was an older girl who lived on the fourth floor of the building next to mine! I sat there for hours and went through every catalogue with my mouth agape. So this is college. I had no idea what image I'd used to represent it in my mind up to that moment, but now that I knew, I saw with my own eyes, it was like I'd bitten the apple. Eve needed to cover up!

I didn't throw the books down the incinerator, maybe for the same reason Brenda didn't. Dreams are too valuable to be burned.

THE BLACKSTONE RANGERS

That next year we all turned fourteen, except for JT, he was fifteen. We started exploring outside the neighborhood more now that we'd learned to hop the 'L'. That's short for elevated train. Chicago has this train system that runs from the southside to the northside and turns into a subway going underground downtown. I guess they figured it was already crowded enough down there without running a train through it. Anyway, one time we were up on B. Heller's roof when we discovered they had an elevated loading dock that allowed trains to roll up and deliver huge containers of spices right to their warehouse. Well, JT figured the tracks must lead somewhere and we should follow them. JT was smart, that's why he was the leader. Anyway, the tracks did lead somewhere, they went right to the L, and all we had to do was jump over to the L's trestle, climb up, and we were on without paying. Cool! After that we went everywhere. We went to Riverview, an amusement park out in the suburbs that we of course learned how to sneak into. We went to Wrigley Field where the Cubs played, but some white boys almost got us with bats one time so we never went back. The best place we went on the 'L' was The Museum of Science and Industry, a huge museum that had everything in it: airplanes, cars, submarines, things showing how power is generated, and homes of the future. It even had a farm inside with fake cows that looked real. One day we were there aimlessly wandering near Paul Bunyan's House when Duh Duh in his infinite wisdom said, "Look at those two white boys over there by themselves, we should rob their asses like those white boys tried to do to us over by Wrigley Field."

"Hell yeah," I chimed in, enjoying the opportunity for mischief.

"Ya'll go around that way," said JT waving me and Woodrow to the back of the house.

"Dino, you and Duh Duh come with me."

We met up on the side of the exhibit with the two poor little white boys caught between us. They were wearing little Izod shirts and penny loafers. We had a nervous gleam in our eyes and saliva on our lips.

"Ya'll got any money," ordered JT in his best tough guy voice.

"No," said the tallest one.

Just then Dino let go with a right uppercut that seemed like it came from his shoe tops. I nearly bit my tongue hoping the sound of that haymaker hadn't set off any alarms. It hadn't, and those two white boys were digging into their pockets like God had just given them the word. The short one had blood all over his mouth from where Dino had just clobbered him, while the tall one kept flinching in anticipation of the left hook he swore was coming. After that, we went back to the museum a few times, but I think we were more terrified of running into those two white boys again than we were emboldened to try and rob anyone else.

That summer a big thing happened that took our minds off of all that kind of stuff. The three neighborhood gangs, The Supreme Lords and The Valiant Lords in the projects, and the Del Vikings across South Parkway were taken over by The Blackstone Rangers. The Stones as they were called, were a citywide operation with ties to the Black Panthers and a huge nationwide syndicate. Chicago's neighborhood gang systems, even The Latin Kings and white gangs were being swallowed up by what would turn out to be the two dominant gangs to this very day, The Blackstone Rangers and The Disciples. One hot day in the middle of June the two uneasy groups of Lords and the really jumpy Del Vikings gathered in Madden Park under the watchful eyes of a group of very hard looking dudes wearing black tams. There was a speech given by the leader who also sported a black armband. It sounded like he was telling them to stop fighting one another and unite to protect their neighborhoods from anyone who would bring harm to their families, namely the Disciples. Then something very interesting happened. Just imagine for a moment your own city block, and how you knew every kid in every house on that block, just like all the Supreme Lords, Valiant Lords and Del

Vikings knew every kid that lived in their hoods. They were instructed to go and get every kid who was at least fifteen and bring him to the park. Victor Jenkins, who was a Supreme Lord, lived in my building. He came over and made Bernard Johnson and Jerome Williams go to the park with him. They lived in my building and they were both sixteen. Leonard Jefferson, who was also a Supreme Lord, lived in the building in front of mine. He got three boys to come to the park with him. He called for Raymond Anthony to come out but his mother wouldn't let him. On their way over to the park Leonard looked at Ervin but he knew if he showed up with a retard they'd dog him out so he settled for the three he had. What happened next was something both terrifying and fascinating. In subsequent years I would glean a number of understandings from what would become a summertime ritual. All the gang members stripped to the waist and stood in two long lines facing each other like a gauntlet. The recruits were also instructed to strip to the waist. Now during all of this the mothers of the recruits are going crazy. There was talk all around about the police but there wasn't a cruiser in sight. The recruits were ordered to walk one at a time down the middle of the two long lines whereupon they were viciously pummeled. If they went down they were kicked and stomped, so needless to say each subsequent inductee learned strategy from those who had gone before. Mothers we'd never seen out of their front windows were running alongside the line in the middle of the baseball field wearing their mu-mu house dresses urging their young men on.

"Come on baby, you can make it, momma is right here." There were gasps of horror and screams every time someone went down amid a flurry of kicks or a kid caught a fist in the face. Boys near the end of the line were yelling encouragement to the lambs they hoped to have a chance to slaughter. When a boy did finally emerge at the other end he was mobbed with the loving arms of the whole neighborhood. People who weren't speaking to you the day before were now running with ice packs and warm towels for your kid's face. Boys who had never gotten so much as a kiss had girls petting them up and offering to dab their wounds. It was like a Civil War battle ground with ghetto nurses running around ministering to their bloodied gangland soldiers. For the first time I saw a neighborhood galvanized into one tight unit. As I stood back and squinted I imagined what an African village must have looked like when their young boys came back from their jungle rite of passage experiences. There was pride, tears of joy, and a long narrow swath of blood running through the infield of Madden Park's baseball diamond. The boys who didn't make it were snatched out by their mothers and with determination taken back to the beginning with the admonition, "you go through there or I'll whip you good!" There wasn't one boy who didn't make it. Hell, all those gangbangers together weren't half the man one momma wuz. The closing ceremony brought tears to my eyes. The Blackstone Rangers brought out three big boxes from which they gave each new member a brand new black tam. With their right fists over their hearts and their new headgear jauntily cocked to the left side, they were sworn in and shouted in unison, "Stone to the bone!" Damn! I couldn't wait till I was fifteen! I've never seen so many black-eyed boys being fawned over before in my life. All summer they strutted around wearing their tams and pinching girls. Even Bernard Johnson who was a wimp now looked radiant and strong and nobody dared mess with him. It didn't matter that his mother had to take him back through the line two times. He was a Stone now, and I swear he looked like a god. His black eye didn't go away for about two months and I later found out that some of the boys were hitting themselves in the eye at night to keep their trophies fresh. Every summer after that the Fourth of July was nothing compared to recruitment day. The streets were blocked off, music blared from every window, picnic tables were up in the park, and all the mothers, aunts, and old ladies were out in their finest nurses regalia. Towels simmered in pots of water on barbecue grills, iodine flowed in abundance, and gifts, gifts like you wouldn't believe were wrapped and waiting for the young boys to become men.

Every culture has its rituals and within these cultures there exist sub cultures, some orthodox, some radical. There in the Ida B. Wells Housing Project we had such a sub culture. Where the dope dealer was our lending institution, the women were our men, and the Blackstone Rangers were our protectors.

As for Raymond Anthony, the boy whose mother kept him from coming out, his sister got raped coming home from school one day, his mother's car had all the tires and battery stolen, and finally somebody threw a Molotov cocktail through their window one night. They moved.

THE MIDDLE PASSAGE

As we got older, so upped the ante. Our basketball games started displaying more skill, especially Dino the show off. He and JT also played on a pony league baseball team that was pretty damn good. It was made up of project boys from our hood and boys from across the park. Me, Woodrow, and Duh Duh would go to their games and talk trash through the fence the whole game.

"Come on Dino get a hit," yelled Woodrow, "the pitcher is a fag. I saw him kissing a boy over at the concession stand."

Then when the pitcher would cut a dirty look our way I'd add, "Boy you know you a fag!"

"Yeah," punctuated Duh Duh.

"Third base, third base," heckled Woodrow, "you hear me talkin' to you fatso, how you gon' run the bases wit' all that booty?" Boy, we'd crack up, and Dino would wind up humiliating them by knocking the ball clean outa sight. We'd really go berserk then.

"Oh my God, you must all be cousins, because there ain't no way any of you would be chosen for a real team," I'd yell, whipping the stands into a frenzy.

Then we'd harmonize, "Go back, go back, go back to the woods, your team ain't nuthin' and your coach ain't no good." At the end of the game we'd stick close to our team and the bat bag because the losers and their relatives would all be spoiling for a fight. Football games were a little different. We had enough boys in my yard and neighboring yards to play some pretty decent games, but nothing was more invigorating than to play boys from other neighborhoods. Every Thanksgiving we played the Gobble Gobble Turkey Bowl against the boys from thirty-seventh street. They weren't especially big or anything, but when you played the boys from your own yard, you knew everybody's tendencies. You knew who to gang tackle, you knew that if you had Dino on your side you were going to win, and you knew who you didn't have to stick if they went out for a long pass, because they were going to drop it. The boys from 37th however were deceptively tricky. They had a couple of little dudes, I think they were brothers or something, that were like weasels. You couldn't get your hands on them long enough to stop them. I remember us lining up on a freezing cold Chicago November morning in Madden Park, which was like concrete with grass, and shouting to one another.

"Dino, you stick the one in the grey, JT take his brother," ordered Hugh Floyd, one of the older guys from the building in back of mine.

"That ain't his brother," JT would yell back.

"Who cares who he is, just don't let him get past you," barks Pritchard Hicks, Hugh's running buddy and a good athlete from my yard.

"Don't worry about my man, you just get the quarterback," returns JT

"Oh his ass is grass and I'm the lawnmower," replied Hicks. He was always saying corny shit like that with his big ass chapped lips. I was always put up on the line to block. Ninety-eight pounds wringing wet and I'm up front looking at the Big Cheese's black greasy ass wearing nothing but sweat pants and a sweatshirt in 35-degree weather.

"Duh Duh, don't you want to stick the Big Cheese?" I pleaded.

"Naw, JT told you to stick him."

"No he didn't, I just like hittin' his big fat ass; he's real slow and I can get some good wood on him, you want to get some?"

"Uh Uh," was his retarded reply. I was gonna be crushed and there wasn't a damn thing I could do about it. Duh Duh was dumb, but he wasn't that dumb. He knew The Big Cheese was gon' hurt me bad and he'd just assume not be anywhere around lest part of the blame fall on him. As they lined up the two little weasels shot furtive glances at The Cheese, and he looked right at me.

"Hey, they're comin' this way," I whimpered over my shoulder.

"Stop em'," JT ordered. I wanted to whine for help, to beg for backup, but of course I couldn't because that would certainly seal my doom for the rest of the afternoon. I thought to myself, all I have to do is fake like I'm going to block him high then dive for his legs, the worst that can happen is he'll fall on me, I'll be crushed to pieces, then rushed to the hospital with a gallant, yet crippling game injury.

At the snap of the ball I yelled, "Going left, going left," which was football talk for somebody get over here and save my ass!

"Hold him up," came a sage reply from somewhere in the remote airways of the secondary. That's all I remember as it seemed the whole offensive line trampled over me. As I lifted one eyeball to witness their team in triumphant end zone celebration, and mine all looking at me as though I were Benedict Arnold, all I could think was that Duh Duh should be laying here instead of me.

MISS VIRGINIA

Ever wonder why most kids are closer to their maternal grandparents than their paternal ones? I think it's because of U.S child custody laws. In some parts of Africa, when a man is done with his wife the children go with the father. After divorce in the United States custody is usually granted to the mother unless she is a total dweeb on drugs, or a cripple or something. My father was born in Atlanta, Georgia. His mother's name was Virginia Jackson (we called her Miss Virginia) and his father's name was William Earl Pettiway (or something funny like that). He had one brother named Pappy. I don't know his real name (I know all my Mom's brothers and sister's names). I was born in 1956 and my brother was born in 1958. After that my father joined the Air Force and my mother had an affair with a bus driver (I think she said his name was Raymond). Anyway, when my father got back from the service my sister popped out a little sooner than his return could explain. He started beating my mom's ass and from that day on Miss Virginia didn't particularly care for her much anymore, and that's why we call my mother's parents granddaddy and grandmamma and my father's mother by her first name.

DRUGS

When I graduated from eighth grade I had the highest reading score in the whole school. I was fascinated with words and how sometimes you could figure out their meanings just by looking at how they were used in sentences. I had been in science fairs, oratorical contests, and spelling bees, but I didn't talk about things I'd done in school when I got home because my boys not only had no interest in stuff like that, but they'd dog me out.

When I got to high school I met this dude named Stevie D. in sheet metal shop. Stevie was slick. He talked about pussy, places he'd been, and music, so you see he had a conversation far beyond what me and my crowd were talking about. The places Stevie D. had been and the things he'd seen were way better than anything we'd ever done. He listened to the Beetles, Jimi Hendrix, Grand Funk Railroad, and groups like that. All we ever listened to was soul music like The Temptations, Al Green, and James Brown. Stevie had been around and I liked him; besides, he was the only dude in the school I knew. Once again my mother had sent me to a different school than all my friends but this time I didn't fight her on it even though I had to walk a whole mile to school. I guess by now I realized my boys weren't getting anything from their school but that same ole' project shit. Besides, all my friends from Mayo had gone to Dunbar so it was natural that I go there too. My boys went to Wendell Phillips, my mother's high school, and the school she named my little brother after. Seems like she'd want me to follow her legacy or something but she didn't. She probably figured it hadn't done her any good, being on welfare and all. I had to take a test to get into Dunbar so I guess that meant you were smart to go there or something. It was a nice school too; newer than Phillips. It had all kinds of shops; that's why it was called a vocational school. You could go there and when you got out you'd be ready for a job. I bet that's what my mother had in mind while she was shoving that nasty cod liver oil down my throat and booting me out into sub-zero weather to walk all that damn way. It was cool though, cause that's where I met Stevie D. He lived on thirty second and Prairie in a bad neighborhood that used to be Del Viking territory, but now it was Stone territory, and even though I wasn't a Stone I lived in the territory so everything was cool. It was Stevie who gave me my first joint. Well, actually it was a big roach but hell I didn't know. I ran home with it and tried to get my boys to smoke with me.

"I don't want none of that crap," snarled JT. So naturally Duh Duh didn't want any either.

"Yeah, that shit slow you down," added Dino. "Damn! Here I done run all the way home with this cool new thing and none of them faggots would smoke any with me."

"You punks," I snarled. "Ya'll don't know everything."

"That shit ain't gonna do nothin' but make you laugh," declared JT

"Yeah," echoed Duh Duh. It didn't make me laugh at all. In fact, I didn't feel anything. At least not then. I started going to Stevie D's crib after school and smokin' my ass off. He'd always give me a joint to walk with and by the time I got to the hood I'd be 'Mellow' and my boys would be like, "Damn, that shit gots to be good!" It wasn't long before we were all smokin' weed. I don't recall how we all got in the groove as much as I remember producing that first joint, but I do know that we were soon "chipping" in on nickel bags and going into the back hallways to roll it and get blasted. Nickels back then were huge. There was this one guy across the park who sold bags through a hole in his bedroom window screen and they were fat! We could get twenty decent joints out of a nickel sack. It didn't take long to move up to pills: Christmas Trees, Black Mollies, Quaaludes, and Acid became regular marijuana condiments.

I introduced Stevie D. to my crowd and he started taking us to concerts with him. By this time my mother had gotten a car and she'd let me borrow it sometimes. While my boys waited around the corner I'd get the car, we'd get totally drugged out, then go to the concert where Stevie would show us the way to sneak in. He knew the way into all the concert halls: The Arie Crown Theatre, The Amphitheatre, and The Auditorium Theatre. The Auditorium was especially fun because we had to climb a fire escape on the side of Roosevelt University, wind our way through the school, and knock on a door that led into the concert hall. Cool!

Somewhere during this time Stevie introduced us to noddin'. Noddin' was an art form. Resplendent with all the nuances of pimpness one could possibly imagine, exceeded only by the subtleness with which it was executed. Subtlety on the mean streets of Chicago was a must, because to get too caught up in the nod could turn you into a slovenly slug subject to being shook-down by the shortest of shorties. Somewhere between wide-awake, eyes-open consciousness, and serious REM sleep is where many sixteen year olds hung out. Our depressant of choice was Robitussin AC. It could be bought over the counter at any drug store; not for long, but for the time being, yes. After you found a cool place to stand, lean, or sit, you'd spend the duration of your high fighting off the gravitational pull of the earth's core working on your eyelids. Your pose was critical because onlookers would have to distinguish between you being hip and high, instead of fucked up and drunk. Man, we did it all: Window Pane, Purple Haze, Orange Sunshine, Organic Mushrooms, Sherman Sticks, Hashish, Panama Red, Acapulco Gold, goddamn! I remember once at a War concert Dino dropped a Purple Micro-dot on the Amphitheater floor with at least ten thousand people on it and found it! Twice! Through all of this, we were still good guys. We hadn't beat up anybody (except push a few white boys around).

CRASH NIGHT

I remember one time me, Stevie D., JT, Dino, Duh Duh, Woodrow's sister Darlene, his woman Latasha, her brother Bill, and another dude from around the crib we called Raimey Boy all snuck in an Earth, Wind, and Fire concert at The Arie Crown Theatre. I remember going through the boiler room and Latasha saying," Damn Lamont, you're a serious cat burglar."

"Hey don't look at me, that dude behind you is the cat," I replied referring to Stevie D. who had taught me everything I knew about the art.

"I'm saying," agreed Darlene who was fine as hell and had Stevie mesmerized.

"I'll take ya'll anywhere you want to go, just hook up with me," said Stevie D. with all the slickness of a cockhound in heat. Once we got inside we all kinda split up because the Andy Fran ushers were in a frenzy. Turns out there was a bumper crop of illegals in the house that night and they were asking people to produce their tickets on the spot. Needless to say, this spooked the hell out of all of us.

"I think we should split up," said JT.

"Yeah," said Duh Duh (as usual).

"I'm going to try to get down on the first floor," said Stevie D.

"Lets go with him," said Bill to Raimey Boy.

"Cool," replied Raimy. "We'll all meet in the lobby after the show okay?"

"That's cool," said JT as he and Duh Duh disappeared.

"What about ya'll," said Stevie referring to Darlene and Latasha.

"We stayin' with Lamont," answered Darlene.

"Yeah," said Latasha sounding a lot like Duh Duh.

"O.k. maybe I'll see you later," Stevie said looking directly at Darlene.

"Oh you will," she replied.

"What the fuck is all this juicy shit about," I demanded.

"Oh chill out Lamont, ain't nothin' but a little sport," Latasha intervened.

"Hey, ain't no biggie, I'm just sayin," I lied. I dug the hell out of Darlene and years later we would hook up. Anyway, me, Darlene and Latasha were walking past the lobby doors and who do we see on the other side going crazy? Woodrow. He's jumpin' up and down imploring me to open the door and let him in.

"Ya'll go on and find a seat," I say to the girls.

"O.k. Lamont, we'll meet here after the show, right?"

"Yeah, now go." I looked around surreptitiously and the Andy Fran, who was looking right at me screams from across the lobby, "Don't open that door!" Woodrow is going out of his mind, I'm easing toward the door with this crazy look in my eyes, and the Andy Fran are coming toward me because they know I'm gonna do it. In a split second I make up my mind as Woodrow sees my conviction and runs toward a far door. In a flash I make a mad lunge for the bar handle and in the same instant Woodrow is in and we hit the 'runnin for your life high gear'. The Andy Fran were on our asses but we were just a little more desperate than they were and in my mind there was no contest.

"See ya," I shouted to Woodrow as I hit an entrance into the auditorium and Woodrow kept going to the next entrance figuring the split second they wasted deciding who to go after would afford us a small window of opportunity to disappear in the darkness. It worked, they went after Woodrow and I eventually found Darlene and Latasha downstairs in some damn good seats.

"Where's Woodie," asked Darlene.

"I don't know, he's in though," I replied.

"What, ya'll split up?" questioned Latasha.

"Had to," I answered. "They were on our ass." We enjoyed the concert which by the way was one of the best Earth, Wind, and Fire had ever performed and afterwards went to the front of the lobby where we were supposed to meet up with the rest of our bunch.

"Where's Woodrow?" asked Latasha.

"Woodrow wasn't with us," answered Duh Duh.

"I let him in," I said, "and the Andy Fran chased us. I got away, but I didn't see what happened to Woodrow."

"There he is," shouted Raimey Boy. Woodrow was outside the lobby doors looking as though he had been in an axe fight and everybody had an axe except him. We all ran over.

"What happened man," asked JT.

"Yeah," said Duh Duh. "Them punks caught me and one of em' beat me with his flashlight."

"I know which door they leave from," said Stevie D.

"Come on, show us where that door is," demanded JT with the Alpha Dog look in his eye. Whenever he had that look we knew there was going to be some serious action.   "Ya'll go home," Dino instructed Darlene and Latasha.

"Well wait a minute," protested Darlene.

"Go home," I seconded as we marched off as to war leaving them standing there like mothers on recruitment day. On the way we saw Courtney and a couple of other guys from the projects and they joined us not wanting to miss out on a rumble, especially against the hated Andy Fran ushers. We waited for about an hour. All the while Woodrow was pacing back and forth like a tiger outside an antelope cage.

"The fag with the flashlight was a little punk too, he just kept jabbing me with it as they man-handled me out the door, I can't wait to smash that punk's face."

"Here they come," someone shouted. We all turned around as a back door opened and about fifteen or twenty Andy Frans walked out.

"Yo bitch what you wanna do now," challenged Woodrow.

"Hey it makes me no never mind," replied one of them. He was medium build, kinda average weight and height.

"Ain't gonna be no ass kickin' as long as I'm around," said one of them brandishing a badge.

"Yeah," said another with a similar piece of tin.

"They're Andy Fran detectives," said Stevie D. "They ain't shit."

"Let em' go head up," said JT from the front of our pack as the two groups faced off in the dark back alley. The detective looked at Woodrow then back at his boy.

"What you wanna do?"

"I took this chump once, I can take him again," was the reply. Woodrow took his coat off and somebody gave him a handkerchief to wrap around his hand.

"Bring yo pussy ass on," he snarled as the Andy Fran handed his uniform to someone to hold. Then it was on. Woodrow lit into that Andy Fran as though his reputation rested on this singular event, which it did. His first two punches landed squarely in the guy's face and were crunchers for sure, but the guy hung in there and countered with an upper cut into Woodrow's stomach that nearly doubled him over and started a mass attack from us. He recovered though and retaliated by kicking the Andy Fran in the balls and when he doubled over polishing him off with a right cross to the jaw that I swore broke his face. The guy managed to grab Woodrow and they wrestled to the ground in a nasty spill. Just then a big brick came from nowhere and smashed the windshield of one of the detective's cars. It should be noted here that bricks don't just fly in from 'nowhere.' They're hurled by antsy co-conspirators who can't stand dancing around a fight like extras in a bad karate movie. I couldn't help it. There was this pristine house brick seemingly placed there by the do-dirty gods with nothing between us but air and bad intentions. It came down with a crash too, sounding like a water tower demolishing a glass house. Everyone jumped, froze, or shitted on themselves before getting their wits back together enough to get the hell outta there.

Woodrow managed to get to his feet, stomp the Andy Fran in the face, and haul ass. The detectives jumped into a car and punched the accelerator. We scurried like rats down the alley which all of a sudden seemed like a death trap. There was a building at the end and seemingly no escape save for a high wall which separated the theatre complex from lake shore drive. We ran for our lives in high gear as the car barreled down on us and doom seemed most eminent. As the car closed in on me and JT we jumped up on the wall grabbing I don't know what because the wall was as smooth and sheer as a plate of glass. We must have found a crack or a small ledge or something because we stuck up there like Spider Man until the car passed us. The car continued down the ally at a ridiculous speed and when Woodrow and Bill put a similar move on them, only then did the driver realize there was a brick wall in front of him and all the brakes in the world weren't going to help. The wall seemed to jump out and chew that car up. Glass shattering, steel crunching, steam belching, and red lights glaring from inside the car seemed to be the only sound in the universe. After a couple of seconds of jaw dropping terror we scurried like rats on a sinking ship over what had only moments before been an unscalable wall . . . Shidd! JT and I found ourselves in the middle of Lake Shore Drive weaving in and out of traffic like we were on an obstacle course. We didn't look back, we didn't stop, we didn't even talk until we got to thirty-fifth street. We were in such shock that when we finally did say something to one another, it wasn't about what we'd just been through.

"That concert was good wasn't it," I asked shakily.

"Yeah, but we done seen them how many times now," implored JT

"I think this is my third time seeing 'em, what about you?"

"Me too," he affirmed.

"We ain't got to see them no more then," I said.

"Hell naw," he agreed.

TOO MUCH TV

It wasn't long after crash night before we started feeling cocky. After mastering the art of sneaking into concerts at will and critically maiming Andy Frans, all we needed was the proper motivation to take the next step. At sixteen with no fathers around to teach us how to be men, we all looked to the older boys as role models. Me, Duh Duh, JT, and Dino never mentioned even having fathers. Woodrow, by virtue of the fact that his father lived with him, at least had someone he could turn to for advice, but the fact that his father was the dope man probably tainted the effect a father figure should have had on his life. We learned sex education and how to treat women from guys who had done the nasty and had been through a few girlfriends. I remember Victor Jenkins, my building's toughest gangbanger and resident lady's man, as the guy I'd learned my first serious female anatomy from. He had the whole JT gang enthralled one afternoon at Madden Park Pool. "You gotta finger em' first so they can get hot. Girls love to be fingered. You use the middle finger because it's the longest," he instructed, holding his middle finger up for inspection as we all held our hands before our faces measuring finger lengths.

"First you play with the clit," he instructed.

"What's a clit," questioned Duh Duh?

"You dumb goof," admonished Dino as he shoved Duh Duh's head, "everybody knows what a clit is."

"Yeah," I said hoping Victor would illustrate what and where a clit was because I didn't have a clue. I don't think Dino did either by the sheepish look on his face.

"Man tell this fool what a clit is," added Woodrow as he leaned in close to listen as well.

"The clit is the little man in the boat," he said as he brought his arm up the way a body builder might to show off his bicep muscle. On the outside of the joint where the upper forearm meets the lower part of the bicep there was a fleshy fold of skin that resembled a pussy slit when Victor squeezed it together.

"See right here," he said pointing to a spot on the upper end of the fold, "this is where the clit sits like a bird in a nest; when you play with him right, he pops his little head out ready to rock and roll."

"Damn," I said almost unconsciously, "so that's how you get a girl hot."

"Hell yeah," affirmed JT, "and after that it's all you."

"Holy shit," said Duh Duh. "I'm gon tear up some ass!" We all slapped hands as Victor sat in our midst like a guru.

All our manhood lessons were learned in similar fashion. From Leonard Jefferson's advice on using Head and Shoulders on your groin area because, "It's all hair man," to Woodrow's brother Jo-Jo showing us how to mix lemonade Kool-Aid with White Port to make 'shake-n-bake schoolboy scotch' that wouldn't leave your breath smelling like alcohol.

Sometimes I really wish I had a father. Like the day Booty Green took my mini bike and my mother had to go across the park with a broom to get it back for me; and probably the day Victor showed up with his new cap.

"Yo, check cool man," said Raimey Boy as Victor strode right into the middle of our baseball game wearing a pair of money green slacks, some green suede shoes, and a really nice green Kangol cap. He looked just like one of the pimps in that movie 'The Mack.'

"You know me, you know me," trumpeted Victor as he broke into his best pimp walk.

"Where'd you get that mean skimmer?" asked JT, referring to Victor's cap.

"Jew town baby, where money on the wood makes bettin' good." We all knew Victor didn't work and his momma didn't have any money.

"Where'd you get the money?" followed Dino.

"We robbed the paper house."

"You lyin'," charged Raimey Boy.

"No I ain't," defended Victor.

"You and who else?" questioned Woodrow.

"Me, Buckwheat, and Leonard," was the reply. The paper house was the little storefront where all the paperboys went after delivering their papers to count the money they'd collected. Since they collected every other Saturday, anyone who hit them would get two week's worth of receipts from about fifteen carriers, which was a nice piece of change if you caught them all together.

"How much ya'll get?" I asked.

"Hundreds my brother, hundreds."

"They must be collectin'" surmised Duh Duh.

"What the fuck you think dufus?" snapped Victor."Man why ya'll have this slow drag wit ya'll?"

"Shut the fuck up Duh Duh," admonished JT. Since Victor was a Blackstone Ranger Main Twenty-One, it would be best to dog Duh Duh out than get on his bad side.

"So what, you all had guns or somethin'?" I asked.

"I had a zip gun, Leonard had a BB rifle, and Buckwheat had a BB pistol that looked just like a real gun; them boys was petrified. We even took Bill's watch." Bill was the man who ran the paper house.

"It was easy as pie wasn't it?" asked Dino.

"Like takin' candy from a baby," was the reply.

Dino's dream of being a big time athlete was fading day by day as his performance in the classroom continued to be more of a joke than reality.

"My brother said it would be easy to rob his job." There it was, Raimey Boy had said it. His brother worked at a well-known burger joint that had 'served over a million' people.

"They've got a guard there," I said.

"You've got to get the drop on him, that's all," offered Victor.

"My mother's boyfriend has a gun," blurted Dino. Silence all around. The only sound was Victor sucking on the toothpick he had in his mouth as he looked from one of us to another.

"What kind," asked Victor, who all of a sudden looked like he had horns sticking out the top of his head.

"It's a Snub Nosed Thirty-Eight," said Dino, "he's a detective." Raimey Boy was the first to come to his senses. "I just mentioned it, but I ain't ready to rob nobody. As a matter of fact, if ya'll through playin' ball, I'm gone."

"Bye," snapped Dino, who all of a sudden was starting to look a lot older, and a lot different.

"He's a punk," snarled Duh Duh.

"Shut the fuck up Duh Duh, you ain't gon' do shit," barked Woodrow.

"I bet I do," countered Duh Duh.

"There ain't never no police up there," said JT. I was shocked, and yet I wasn't. I should have been scared but it seemed curiosity was the prevailing emotion.

"Why don't we go talk to Raimey Boy's brother and get the scoop," I reasoned. "That would be the logical thing to do," said a suddenly smart Duh Duh. We all just looked at him with our mouths open and then suddenly burst out laughing. Duh Duh laughed too because he knew he wasn't supposed to be saying words like 'logical.'

We found Raimey Boy's brother and he told us that there would be money in both cash registers and that Friday night's receipts would be the largest. We talked about it, and smoked on it a couple of days until Friday came and it was time to put up or shut up. Dino was ready.

"So we gonna do this or what?"

"It don't make me no never-mind," replied Woodrow. "What about you JT?" With all eyes riveted on him, JT made the decision that would change our lives forever, especially Dino's.

"Man, as broke as I am I'm game for anything, can you get the piece Dino?"

"Yep, my mother and her boyfriend are both sleep right now."

"Well go get it and meet us back in Lamont's hallway," he instructed, "and hurry up!" Dino took off like Jim Brown in the Dirty Dozen, and when we got to my hallway he was already there.

"Check it out," he said as he pulled the piece from his jacket. It was a sweet blue steel snubnose with a wooden handle.

"Let me check it out," I said slightly sticking my tongue out impressed by its heft. "Oh hell yeah, let me swing this bitch," I insisted.

"What are you gon' do?" asked JT

"I know what to do, anybody else want to do it?" There were no takers so the job was mine.

When we got there Woodrow stayed out on Pershing Road to give a whistle if any cops came. Duh Duh was outside the restaurant door to relay any warning Woodrow might give. Me, JT, and Dino went inside. Dino and I stepped up to the window as if we were going to order, and I drew on the guard.

"Pull your piece out of the holster with two fingers," I instructed, looking him in the eye. "Place it on the counter and slide it to me with one finger." A technique I'd seen on television. Dino and JT jumped gayly over the counter and started rifling the registers. I pulled the guard's piece to me. It was a huge nickel plated Smith and Wesson .38 Special! I kept my eye on the guard until my boys were finished, then we broke out of there as if our asses were on fire. We sprinted across Pershing Road and disappeared into the dark projects like The Shadow. We split the money five ways which was about three hundred dollars each and got high. Since I took the guard's gun it was mine, but I sold it to Dino that night for $50 dollars.

THE QUIET ONES

Dino was a private person. He never talked about his family's business, his siblings, or anything like that. You didn't knock on his door either. There's an interesting dynamic among project dwellers. You see, there are a lot of people stacked literally on top of each other and one would think there'd be few secrets between them, but that wasn't necessarily the case. There were loud families whose business everybody knew, and "Grand Central Station" cribs where all the kids hung out. Then there were families like Dino's that were as benign and unremarkable as a toenail. There were six very well groomed kids and JoAnn his mother. She never came out, the kids never left the front yard (although I did play a lot of Doctor with his oldest Sister), and nobody seemed to notice or bother them. Dino and his older Brother were good athletes, the two girls were polite and good doubledutch ropers, and the two youngest Boys were as quiet as church mice.

So when Dino disclosed his Mother had a boyfriend I for one put that down in my mental rolodex, and when he said the guy was a detective I couldn't even wrap my mind around it. How the hell did he get in? I'd never seen a soul who didn't live in Dino's building go in there! I was stupefied, and when Dino produced a gun I just about fainted. The kinda chubby, light skinned woman with six deep chocolate kids has a boyfriend? That day was a turning point for me, but I think for Dino it was the day he clicked out of being the neighborhood athlete and clicked into being something else. Unnoticeable and unannounced, it's the quiet ones you have to watch out for.

DINO, DUH DUH, AND THE CRAP KINGS

The human brain is an amazing thing. It can not only adapt its learning style to different stimuli, but it can also re-program itself entirely like one of those scary super-computers in the movies. Just like in laboratory mice when their brain experiences a shock in a certain corridor of a maze they don't go down that corridor again, ever. I know because that's what happened to Dino. Once he realized he was never going to be a star athlete, and possessed no academic aptitude, his brain re-programmed itself. He no longer carried a ball with him everywhere or based his priorities around sporting engagements. He had said, "to hell with it", and his brain re-programmed itself to make Dino one of the slickest hustlers in the jects.

One day we were just hangin' out doing nothing in particular when Dino noticed Duh Duh clicking a pair of dice between his fingers and shaking them.

"Where you going with those dice Duh Duh?" goaded Dino.

"I'm fixin' to go break me some niggahs up on thirty-ninth. You didn't know I was a young hustler, did you?"

"Niggah YOU don't know you a hustler," scoffed JT, as he smacked Duh Duh on the back of his head.

"Boy, you talk like a fool," quipped Duh Duh as he quickly shook the dice, broke down on one knee, and threw them out.

"Stang 'em," he shouted as seven rolled up big as day.

"A dollar says you can't do that again," challenged Dino as he dug into his khakis for a bill.

"Put your money on the ground so I can get on down," rhymed Duh Duh as we all looked first with amazement as Dino pulled out a rare buck, then at Duh Duh as he clicked the dice around in his fingers setting them up before he blew on them and let 'em fly. "Break his heart," Duh Duh shouted just as he snapped his fingers. Seven. "Next," snapped Duh Duh as he snatched Dino's dollar from the pavement.

"Two dollars says you can't do it again," dared JT as he dug into his pockets. By this time Woodrow and I were elbowing each other for viewing position.

"Move Lamont, you ain't got no money," said Woodrow.

"How do you know what I've got?" I reasoned.

"Show me," he challenged.

"I ain't got to show you shit," I said, about to burst into laughter. Duh Duh threw his two dollars onto the ground and so did JT

"Let me see them dice," demanded JT. Duh Duh handed them over.

"You know I ain't gon' cheat you JT, I'm gon' take your jack fair and square." JT handed the dice back after a thorough inspection. Duh Duh clicked them over a few times, blew, and threw.

"Rip!" shouted Duh Duh. Seven, again.

"Damn boy, you been practicin'," cried Dino as we all murmured in agreement and Duh Duh snatched up his winnings.

"I can do this shit in the dark, what do you think I do up in that creepy hole all day?" Dino was really geeked-up now.

"That's all good, but can you pick up points?"

"Hell yeah, especially nines, sixes, and eights," said Duh Duh.

"Well let's shoot some dice goddammit, we ain't gon just stand around and let Duh Duh pick us clean, are we?" I said trying to take the dice from Duh Duh.

"Hell yeah, let's tick to see who goes first," said Woodrow, "give up the dice Duh Duh." Each player then tossed one die and the one with the highest number showing got to start the game with the next highest number going after he fell off and so on down the line. Dino threw a five and got to go first. He threw a four which was his 'point,' and he had to throw that again before throwing a seven to win.

"Foe little Joe come to me baby," was Dino's incantation as he hopped the dice out of his hand as though he was playing ball and jacks. Seven.

"Git yo awkward shooting ass back before you lose all your money," bellowed Woodrow as he snatched up

Dino's cash and the dice. "Watch a shark in motion. Who got me faded?"

"I'll fade you," I said throwing down a dollar. "I need some money." We shot dice until holes started wearing into the knees of our jeans. Every few minutes someone would walk up and join the game until we had a large circle of yelling, drinking, shit talkin' hustlers all trying to emerge with a fat pocket.

"Man hurry up and fall off so I can get the dice," spat Papa Hard, a short husky gangbanger from across the park.

"Nigga if I don't hit ain't a Jesus," exclaimed Dino as he let the dice fly. "Eight skate come donate, give me my damn money," he shouted when his point eight rolled over. By now there was quite a bit of cash on the ground and in the fists of the participants, and in hindsight we should have thought to slide our big bills into our back pockets and keep only the chump change out in the open.

"Don't nobody fuckin' move, this is a goddamn stick up!" I'd seen the two rough looking dudes join the circle and figured they'd get in on the action when they could. I guess they were figuring the same thing.

"Just put all the money on the ground," they demanded, "and nobody will get shot." One of them had a big pistol and the other one had a sawed-off shotgun he'd pulled from under his jacket. They collected everything, the money on the ground, from our fists, and even a couple of watches and a pair of Chuck Taylors. When they left a dude named Sammy who lived on thirty-seventh street said, "As many crap games as I've been in I ain't never thought of stickin' em' up."

"That way you're a winner every time," murmured Dino.

THE END OF INNOCENCE

That summer we all turned sixteen. Except for JT, he was seventeen. And all of a sudden we stopped bringing our baseball gloves out with us. We just came out... looking. You know how some days you get up in the morning and don't have a clue what direction you'll head that day? Well, most of our days were like that now. In magazines there were all these happy images of dads playing basketball in the driveway with their sons. We didn't have no driveway, no ball, and no daddy. You switch on the tube and there are dads teaching their sons how to set a hook in a fish's mouth, or how to take a proper swing at a baseball. All the bats we ever had were beat up pieces of stick-shit we'd found somewhere or managed to steal from the Y.M.C.A. in our pant legs. Nobody ever taught us anything.   When we woke up in the morning, we went outside to our daddy ... daddy streets. The hood taught us everything we needed to know to survive. Instead of a father teaching us how to run and jump, the police taught us that. We knew how to low run. That's running in a crouch to minimize mass, disguise your height, and take advantage of parked cars as concealment. We learned to hit fences at the highest point possible, do a marine flip over the top, and hit the 'crete running on the other side. We could jump real good. The point is, these were critical times in our lives and we had nobody there to take us through. There were no structured activities, cultural outings, or bonding experiences for us. Just put on your jeans, go outside, and there you'd find six or seven other wards of the state eager to begin their lesson in Street Knowledge 101. We'd find out who was there and who we'd have to go and get even though we didn't like to go to people's houses because most times it was too embarrassing. Nobody wanted you looking into their fucked-up crib. Pissy ass babies running all over the place, raggedy ass furniture with big stank spots all over it and the stuffin' hangin' all out. The funk of a thousand days and nights of pent-up poverty rolling out of the apartment like some stifling fog that makes your eyes water. Heaven forbid if you saw their momma. Nobody had beauty parlor money, so if you were jerk enough to go up to somebody's crib you deserved whatever you saw. A lot of dude's mommas were overweight and waddled their fat, smelly asses to the door wearing what seemed to be the universal po' project woman's garb, a housedress that looked like one of those hospital gowns only with the back closed. Their hair was always frazzled and they had hard, crusty, ashy feet with toenails from hell and seemingly a stain from every meal they ever cooked on that damn housedress. Nobody wanted you to see their momma 'cause later on playin' the dozens you'd have ammunition. Sometimes big momma would have a beer, a cigarette, or both in her hands and a trusty seat, usually at a window or in their favorite sunk-in spot on the couch. They didn't give a damn either. Years since the last man came calling they're long past trying to be presentable. All you could do was try to avert your eyes and play it off like you're quite comfortable breathing shallow. Most times we'd simply yell up to the window or if they lived on the first floor, go to their bedrooms and knock on the screen.

A dude could be one of the baddest cats in the jects with much respect from all the fellas, but if you ever went to his crib all that went out the window. The baddest dudes turned humble as hell and you were instantly taken into an unspoken confidence that was both powerful and uncomfortable. You knew something that no one else knew. You saw his younger siblings all dirty and unkempt. You saw the big sister looking like a street tramp working the curling iron on the stove, popping her gum, getting ready to be gone all night leaving her kids for big momma to watch. And if your timing was good you got to see big brother the heroin addict from hell blow through on one of his flights... begging, grabbing change purses, patting down everybody in the house with the wildest eyes and fiercest visage ever. Once outside your boy, now reduced to a shameful pulp, curses the disgrace of the preceding scene and indirectly justifies any and all resulting behavior on his part.

Many people are scared to come into the projects because they say it's too bad there. The fact is none of us were vicious bad. We were happy kids who didn't know we were poor. We didn't know we were damaged goods, and we certainly didn't know there was a vacuum of despair that would suck the playful twinkle from the eyes of children growing up there. Once we turned sixteen and the realization of hopelessness reared its ugly head, once our brains began to reprogram themselves, and once we had played into the hands of the ghetto mentality, we became something else, something frightening, something none of us saw coming.

T BAY
OR
WHEN A PARTY ISN'T A PARTY

A child doesn't have a true concept of death . . . not really.

No one ever dies in cartoons and most kids have both parents, grandparents, and everyone they ever knew still alive. A child has never heard the word mortality. Someone going to heaven or hell is strictly allegorical and besides, everyone knows kids are bulletproof. Right?

"I know where there's a house party" said Dino.

"Where?" inquired Woodrow.

"You know that girl Jack O? . . . her crib," replied Dino with choked smoke tumbling out of his mouth. I looked over at Wood; even JT seemed interested. We'd been holed up in Wood's room smoking weed for three albums now and squeezin' up on some honeys didn't sound too bad. Only thing was, Jack O lived across the park, old Valiant Lords' territory.

"She live right there on Rhodes don't she?" examined JT.

"Yep, right at the gate," stated Dino matter-of-factly.

"Not at the gate," Woodrow warned. "She's like in the middle of the block."

"Not far from the gate," defended Dino.

"Not close either" returned Woodrow.

"Let's go!" bounced Duh Duh.

"I don't know." I cautioned, "they don't party over here and we don't party over there."

Dino gave me a look of skepticism, "Okay, so we don't go hanging out with them and they don't make a habit of hanging out over here, but we go through there to Jewels all the time, and Levy and his boy was just over here last night in Peaches' hallway or is you forgettin?"

It's true I go right through there...kinda, to go to Jewels the neighborhood grocery store. I skirt around the edges of their territory giving them a lot of respect even though we all supposed to be Stones now, and Levy, who's also a Stone now, was definitely hanging out in Peaches' hallway last night.

"I say we hit that bitch," stumbled Duh Duh.
Nobody paid him any attention.

"Jack O is thick and I saw her the other day in a car full of fine chicks," added Dino.

"Oh hell yeah," backed Woodrow, "let's go!"

"Wait a minute, wait a minute," cautioned JT. "All five of us just bustin up in there, how that's gon look?"

"Right" I reasoned. "So we'll let Duh Duh go in first; they know he's harmless." Duh Duh gave me a quizzical look but he was too dumb and high to put it together.

"Then me and Dino will go in, hell everybody loves Dino, he ain't gon' have no problem getting in. Then a few minutes later you and Woodrow can come in. They all know Wood is Papa D's Son and your brother is former Supreme Lord royalty, ain't nobody gon mess with you." JT cradled his chin in his hand looking thoughtful while we all waited for him to work it out in his head. He dropped his hand and twisted his mouth like he'd had a stroke. "If we get fucked up I'm fuckin you up Dino."

"If we get fucked up you'll be too fucked up to fuck me up," wisecracked Dino while bopping his head from side to side.

Everybody simultaneously started 'fixin' to go. I took one last super drag on the joint and passed it to Woody. Duh Duh grabbed his coat still trying to figure out why he was going in first while Dino was looking at his gym shoes trying to map his strategy because there was snow on the ground outside.

We crossed Madden Park with a full moon lighting up the projects like one of them flares they use in the army. Dino stayed on the sidewalk to protect his shoes and had to exit through the gate. The rest of us cut straight over the ice rink slipping and sliding and exited through a hole in the fence on the used-to-be Valiant Lord side (we had an identical hole on our side). It was good that it was Winter because that meant no bangers were hanging around downstairs scrutinizing the five of us approaching the building.

"All right Duh Duh hit it," ordered JT, and without a word Duh Duh obediently pushed through the downstairs door and disappeared into 'Holy Ghost' by the Bar Kays. A few minutes later me and Dino went in and just like I said he got respect right away. "What up D." Booty Green was right at the door. I didn't make eye contact with him.

"You playin tomorrow?" Pumpkin (I could see him as a chubby little baby being called Pumpkin by his mother), a Blackstone Ranger, was inquiring about the next day's hockey game out on the ice. Boys from thirty-eighth played boys from thirty-ninth, thirty-seventh, and across the park. Tomorrow would be us against the boys from across the park. There was no hockey equipment really. Everybody had skates (mostly figure skates) and a stick, but no goalie pads. The boys used baseball catcher's equipment and a baseball glove. It was kinda funny but the games were competitive nonetheless.

"Yeah I'll be there baby," smiled Dino and gave Pumpkin five (a hand slap for the hip impaired). After Woody and JT got in we were all good. I saw this girl I knew named Baby. Nobody knew her real name, and stuff like that didn't matter in the jects. Nobody knew your 'government' name unless they were in your class at school.

"What up Baby."

"Hey what up Mont, long time."

"Yeah, you lookin good." I was movin into pimp mode now.

"Thank you, you too." She played along.

"Wanna dance?"

"Yeah, we can do that." I guess Baby was about 16 or 17, smooth chocolate skin, nice titties sittin up there and a plump juicy ass. We started doing the bump then Baby said, "Double that thang up." and we went right into the double bump. I was bouncing off her soft hips. At one point I noticed my Johnson (penis, for you know who) was rock hard. I had to refocus on the music and off Moby. In fact, when the song ended I decided to take a break from Baby to calm my shit down or it could be embarrassing. Slow dancing was out of the question.

"Which way is the bathroom," I asked Baby. I already knew where the bathroom was, all the apartments were basically the same, asking was just my exit line.

"Right down that hall," she pointed.

"Thanks." Whew, a clean getaway I thought to myself as I made my way through the crowd. The last thing I wanted was to be walking around with a massive woodie. The bathroom was at the end of a hallway that had three bedrooms on it. The last bedroom before the bathroom was like a coatroom where everybody had piled their coats on the bed. As I walked by my eyes were instantly drawn to several purses on the floor pushed slightly under the bed to offer some concealment. I didn't hang around too long drawing attention to myself but my mind was completely corrupted and I wanted to know how many purses were in there. I went in the bathroom and closed the door, my mind racing. As many purses as I saw, there had to be some money in there. The party was raging and as I stood there at the mirror there was no traffic down the hall. Piece of cake.

I went back out into the party and found Woodrow.

"Yo, go down that hall and tell me what you see."

"What the hell you talkin bout," asked Wood suspiciously.

"Just walk to the end of the hall, turn around and come back." Woody looked at me devilishly with the corners of his mouth curling into a sly smile, looked around to make sure no one was looking, then eased down the hall like he was on silent roller skates. I didn't watch him but instead watched everyone else. He came back silently over my shoulder.

"All them damn purses and shit in that room," he whispered.

"Ain't that some shit," I whispered out the corner of my mouth still watching the crowd.

"Go get JT," I murmured. Before long we were all huddled in a corner pretending to sip punch and point at girls. In reality we were plotting to ease into the room much like we had eased into the party and raid pockets and purses.

Duh Duh said, "So when I go into the room do I close the door behind me?"

"Naw just stand there like you're in front of a firing squad you goof ball," JT said as he gave Duh Duh the duh face. "Hell yeah close the door, quietly." JT just shook his head from side to side. I'm sure he was wondering why we brought Duh Duh in the first place.

We were so stealth, one at a time standing on the corner of the hallway until we blended into the wall and then invisibly like mist, drifted into the room. Once we were all together we locked the door and rifled through that stuff like migrant farm workers separating wheat from the chaff. Only Duh Duh was stopping to look at stuff.

"Is this a fingernail clipper or a knife?" he asked JT.

"Put that shit down and get to work you fool or I'm gon' smack you upside the head," JT whispered.

"Okay okay," responded Duh Duh with a goofy smile on his face. Just then the doorknob turned loudly and we all froze stock-still.

"Is this the room to put my coat?" a female voice shouted back into the music. "Yeah, it's open," came the faint reply. The knob was turned again this time with some shaking.

"It's locked," the voice shouted with annoyance.

"It ain't locked, just..." The knob was tried again as we looked at JT, the door, the window, the closet, inside our souls. Oh shit.

"Who's in there?" came an adult sounding male voice as the door was pounded on. JT who was by the window pulled up the shade and opened it. A biting winter gust rushed in as we noisily scrambled to look out at just how long a drop it would be to the ground.

"We gotta get the hell outa here," spat a suddenly emergent leader Duh Duh. We were on the second floor, and while it wasn't a dangerously ridiculous proposition, it wasn't a diving board jump either. It was a long way down.

"I'll go first," blurted Woodrow.

"Hurry up," I said. I was scared to death of being beat up in these people's house. They were gang bangers who knew how to inflict pain. Woodrow ambled out of the window, hung on the sill and then let go. I watched him fall to the ground and it became evident that what looked like soft snow was in reality a sweet drift covering rock hard two degree below zero dirt just like we played football on. Wood grimaced and somehow dragged himself up and started to limp-run to the hole in the fence. Dino and JT jumped and then I went. I didn't want to let go of that ledge, but it sounded like everybody at the party was pounding on the bedroom door and I could feel the room concuss with every lunge to open it. I wanted to close my eyes and let go but thought better of it lest I land awkwardly and sprain my ankle. So I looked down, pushed out a little and let go. It seemed like forever before I hit the ground. It was so damn hard I was sure my ankles, my knees, and all my intestines were destroyed and there was no way I'd ever get up.

"Get out of the way!" Duh Duh shouted from above me. I heard a mighty crash as the bedroom door was kicked in and saw Duh Duh coming towards me. I rolled out of the way just as he piled into the ground and fell onto me. That's just what I needed, more pain.

"You mutha fuckas," came the distressed roar from the window as me and Duh Duh stumbled toward the street. Woody, Dino and JT were in the park when I looked up. "Shit, let's go," I screamed as me and Duh Duh desperately tried to make our bodies do what we wanted. As we hit the hole in the fence I swore I heard gunshots crack the still night air. 'Pow, pow' damn, it WAS gun fire.

"Shit they're shooting," I screamed at Duh Duh and hit the running for your life high gear.

We ran across that ice like wintertime jackrabbits. Blackstone Ranger 'One Love' was out the window (no pun intended) and bullets were whizzing by plinking onto the frozen surface all around us. It seemed like every one of them fools had a gun and was shooting their asses off. A bullet hit the swing post as I ran past it and I swore I would die that night. Then a funny thing happened. It seems some boys on our side of the park were hanging out in my hallway, heard the shots, and had come out to investigate. When they saw us running and being shot at they pulled out guns and started shooting back. Now there were bullets flying every which way with muzzle flashes, boys scrambling behind cars, straight chaos. We ran right through our boys shooting, past my hallway, all the way to Peaches' hallway seemingly before taking one breath. When me and Duh Duh got there the look on everybody's faces was one of pure terror. We'd never been through anything like that before and our emotions were in overload.

"I'm fucking you up Dino," said JT trying to catch his breath.

"Me too." I said.

"We all fuckin you up," added Woodrow.

"Going in that room was your idea Mont, we wouldn't never went in there if it wasn't for your thieving ass," blamed Dino.

"Yep," joined Duh Duh. Just then T Bay and One-Eyed Jack busted up in the hall.

T Bay was the youngest of three Mosby brothers who lived in J T's building. They were all younger than we were with T Bay being eleven, twelve tops. He was just a kid but his moms was an alcoholic, his two uncles were alkies too and there was no father so needless to say he and his brothers were always on the street fending for themselves. There were a lot of kids like that in the Jects. They grew up fast, grizzled early, and always appeared older than they really were. They were breathing hard.

"What the fuck happened?" screamed One-Eyed Jack.

Everybody spoke at once:

"Dino took us into Valliant Lord territory"

"Mont tried to get us killed"

"We just didn't think things out that's all"

"These some dumb mutha fuckas

"I don't know"

"It's fucked up man," said JT. "We shouldn't have been over there in the first place, it's our own damn fault."

T Bay half sat half collapsed on the stairs and One-Eyed Jack slid down beside him.

"Well, all I know is they was definitely trying to pop ya'll's ass and that's the truth. They came all the way to the middle of Vernon and you never see no shit like that."

"Who was that shooting back at 'em," asked JT.

"Victor, Leonard, and Bernard were the main ones, we wasn't sticking around to take no attendance." T Bay let out a little wimpy laugh, which was unusual for him because he was always busting out laughing. Just then I noticed him holding his side. I walked over to him, "Move your hand T Bay you hiding something?" T Bay slowly moved his hand revealing a deep red spot on his military issue field jacket.

"Is this blood T Bay?" Now everybody got up and came over.

"Move your hand," ordered JT. T Bay slowly moved his hand again as JT unzipped the jacket revealing a big red blood spot on T Bay's thick green cardigan sweater.

"Oh man exclaimed Woody, you're hit T Bay!" JT unbuttoned the sweater and gingerly pulled up his tee shirt showing a whole lot of blood.

"Damn," Dino cried out, T Bay is shot!" I've never witnessed such a pall sweep over a place like the dark cloud that descended upon that hallway. Now T Bay was taking short, labored breaths.

I spoke first. "If the police come they gon want to talk to all of us. We're not just witnesses, they're gonna say we wuz in it." We all silently looked from one to the other. I swear I heard my heart pounding inside my chest.

"I'm outa here." One-Eyed Jack blew out of that hall like his ass was on fire. We all remained silent, looking for an answer, a sign that would tell us what to do. For once we didn't look to JT.

"Let's get the fuck out of here." Duh Duh started backing toward the door.   "Wipe shit off that you touched," instructed JT and make sure you ain't drop nuthin."

Dino cracked the hallway door and looked out, "Let's go now," he said in a half whisper and we all backed out of the hall giving T Bay one final look.

Not only did we never tell a soul what went down that night, we never spoke about it among ourselves. It was like this deep dark secret that would come to life if we ever brought it up. Victor, Leonard, and Bernard not only didn't speak to us for a long time, they hardly looked at us if we crossed paths in the jects. Nobody ever came up to me and said they were emptying the garbage that night or they'd heard this or that ... nothing.

None of us went to T Bay's funeral services.

DUH DUH DIRTY DANCIN'

That next summer Woodrow and I got lifeguard jobs and started having sex. JT lucked up and got a job at the Post Office and started making real money. Dino and Duh Duh couldn't swim, so they couldn't take the lifeguard test, and they were too dumb to pass the Civil Service exam so they just kept on doing what they were doing. We worked down on 31st Street Beach, where there was a beach house that had locker rooms, a first aid office, boat rooms and an abundance of places you could go with a girl and have some privacy. What had seemed so complex up until then was really very simple once you put on that guard uniform. Girls would hang out all day and deep into the night giggling and letting their swimsuit straps fall down and stuff like that. After the beach officially closed we'd take them into the beach house and do the nasty. We were in heaven.

We weren't the only ones getting flavor though. One night we were all sitting around drinking beer when a brand new Buick Electra 225 pulled up and Duh Duh got out.   "Hell naw," cried Dino, "you didn't tell me chick was pushin' a Deuce and a Quarter."

"With velour seats and tilt steering wheel," returned Duh Duh as he snatched a cold one from the bag.

"Wait a minute, wait a minute," demanded JT, "you got a girl and you ain't told me nothing about it?"

"Hey, you been at work while I'm out here on the streets doin' thangs," said Duh Duh while slappin' five with Dino.

"There's a whole lot you don't know."

"Nigga don't get cocky, I'll still warm yo' ass up," threatened JT.

"Naw man we still down, but this broad is fine J.T.," replied Duh Duh.

"I'm diggin' her man and she digs me."

"Where you meet her Duh Duh," asked Woodrow.

Duh Duh sat down on the stoop and we all leaned right in as usual. "I was at the record store with Dino when I saw her checkin' me out. I was clean too man. I had just got my new tailor made walking suit from Sunbeam's, I had my Kangol cocked ace-deuce, and these hard Bally gators I got on now. She was bold too man, she just kept looking me right in the face, hell, I had to say something. So I did. I walked over to her and said, "Yo what's your name?"

"You goof ball," I said as I smacked him upside the head, "is that all you could think of to say?"

"Yeah man," said Duh Duh.

"So what did she say?" asked Woodrow.

"She said, 'My name is Linda.' I said my name is Raymond, my friends call me Duh... Ray. 'Hi Ray, what are you buying?' Oh, I ain't buying nothing, I'm just showing my boy over there what to get. She said, 'What, he don't know what the hip tunes are?' Naw, he need me to show him what's up."

Duh Duh was acting it all out; moving from the left side to the right, changing his voice from his hip self to a sweet high-toned falsetto representing the girl.

"So she said, 'Oh is that right?' Yeah, I guess you could say I know my way around. 'Is that right?' That's right, you need me to show you some things? Then she said, 'Maybe.' Then I came strong. When you want me to start?"

Duh Duh was getting carried away now making up stuff that was so far from the truth it wasn't even funny.

"Then she said, 'well, seeing as how you all busy with your boy and everything.' I couldn't let her get away so I dogged Dino, busy what? I ain't busy, what you want to do? 'Well my car is parked outside, you want to go for a ride?' Baby, you ain't said nothin' but a W (a word for the hip impaired), let's go."

"Boy you must think we stupid," said Woodrow.

"He ain't lying," returned Dino, "tell them the rest." We leaned in even more.

"So, we went out to her car and . . . man! She was driving that long, clean ass Deuce. Boy look, I jumped in that bitch and cocked to the side like I was Willie Dynamite. We spun over to the lickka stow, picked up some Crown, went to the lake, and it was on like popcorn!"

"Get the fuck outa here," I exclaimed.

"If I'm lyin, I'm flyin," declared Duh Duh with his right hand in the air as if he were swearing an oath.

"And you didn't come and tell me?" uttered JT in disbelief.

"Your boy lost his cherry and you weren't even there," I said as we all cracked up.

"She popped that thang wide open," affirmed Duh Duh proudly.

After that Duh Duh and his new lady went everywhere together. They'd pull up at the beach and park while me and Woodrow watched them smooch from our lifeguard chairs. Duh Duh and Dino's hustling picked up noticeably now that Duh Duh had a woman to sport. He was crazy about this chick and nobody could tell him anything anymore. One day Duh Duh pulled up in the Deuce without Linda.

"Oh you sportin' the Deuce regular now huh?" asked Woodrow.

"You know you ain't got no license," I added.

"Pimps don't need license," was his reply.

"So where you been man," I asked.

"I been staying out at Linda's crib," Duh Duh replied proudly.

"Boy you done hit the big time ain't you?" I pointed out.

"Naw, she's just getting some big bone that's all," laughed Duh Duh.

Then Woodrow came out of left field and blew us all completely away. "Yo Duh Duh, I was telling Papa D about this chick Linda you've been running around with and he said Jo Jo used to run syrup with a dude named Parker, and that Parker had a transvestite brother named Leonard who drove a green Deuce and lived up on Rush Street. What street Linda live on?"

It seemed an eternity before Duh Duh asked, "What's a transvestite?"

"That's when a faggot gets silicone titties and has a sex change to become a bitch," replied Woodrow flatly. I looked at Woodrow in disbelief. I couldn't fathom why he would bust out with some shit like that. Out of all of us Duh Duh was the least able to handle emotional pressure. His whole life had been one big stress tab and now Woodrow was laying this heavy drama on him?

I looked at Duh Duh, "you've seen the pussy, I mean, it's a regular pussy right?" Duh Duh just stood there in a cleaver tailor made walking suit, his Kangol perched jauntily to one side, kids playing in the background, an ice cream truck's merry melody in the faint airways of our minds with his mouth open. He looked as though he had just been shot by his best friend and was in shock before falling to the ground.

"She . . . she don't live on Rush Street," was all he could utter.

"So what, ya'll' gon' work, or turn in them goddamn uniforms?" came the beach Captain's voice jolting us back to reality.

"Yo man check that out," urged Woodrow as we backed our way onto the beach and Duh Duh sleepwalked over to the car blinking as if he'd just seen a ghost.

"Where did you get that shit from," I attacked Woodrow.

He looked me right in the eyes and asked, "did you see the look on his face?"

ME, JT & SUGAR
THE SHOOTING GALLERY

The more time we spent hangin out at Woodrow's, the more of Papa D's people we came into contact with. One of those people was Sugar. I remember when I was a youngster I used to see Sugar downstairs in back of Woodrow's building. He was the stop soldier. If anybody came to Papa D's to pick up a package, Sugar would take care of them before they got upstairs. This served two purposes. One of course was to keep the house traffic down to a minimum, and the other was if a bust went down Sugar would take the fall and not Papa D. I remember times when he'd come upstairs to drop off money and re-stock on product. I asked him one day, "Yo sugar, ain't nobody ever jumped you out there?"

"Hell yeah," was his reply, "but both them dudes ain't around no more," as he continued to count his cash.

I remember one time me, JT, and Woodrow were runnin' the crib. I was working the door, while Woodrow counted money that came in from the street. JT was rolling joints, playing records, and generally keeping me and Wood happy while we did work. There was a knock at the door and it was Sugar. "What's up little brothers," he said with a smile.

"Ain't nothin' Sugar, what's up with you," said Woodrow getting the keys out to open the gate on the door.

"I need to get out and do a little somethin' today, any one of you brothers got a car?"

"You ain't workin today?" I asked.

"Naw man, Bruno is doin' his thang with my spot." What he really wanted to say was that Woodrow's older brother had taken his place downstairs but wasn't sellin shit, he was shootin' up all the dope instead. Bruno and Jo Jo were straight up dope fiends living in heroin heaven. Papa D constantly told Sugar not to let Bruno do that, but what was 150-pound Sugar gonna do with 250-pound Bruno who was the big man's son?

"You know I got a car Sugar, don't be comin' up here playin' dumb," replied JT as they slapped hands giving each other five.

"Check it out," Sugar began, "I got some sweet game out there. I'll cut you in and show you a few moves while we're at it. All I need is a driver." JT twisted his lips in thought the way he always did but we knew he was gonna do it. The first reason was that he always wanted to be in on anything juicy, and secondly he wasn't going to let us see him punk out.

"How much you think I can make?" With that question we knew JT was in.

"About a hundred," was Sugar's reply.

Shidd, JT was getting his coat and so was I.

"Can I go too?" I asked.

"I only need one driver," replied Sugar.

"I know," I said. "I just want to go for the ride."

"Ain't no thang," answered Sugar, and we were out.

"You got it Wood?" asked JT.

"Yeah man, ya'll go ahead," replied Woodrow as he licked a joint. Sugar instructed JT to get on the Dan Ryan Expressway then hit the Eisenhower and head out West. Soon we reached Sugar's first stop.

"Pull over here and just wait for me, I'll only be a minute." It was a liquor store and we thought maybe he wanted a taste to stay warm because it was a little nippy outside. When he came back he didn't have a bag in his hand.

"Where's your taste," asked JT?

Sugar just laughed. "Here it is."

He pulled from his coat a fifth of Crown Royal, then another, and another, and another.

"Damn," we both said in unison. "Where did you have all of that?"

"I'm gon' show you, but let me flex a little while before I show you the art." And show us he did. We must have stopped at twenty liquor stores, and out of every one he lifted at least three or four big bottles of expensive stuff. He was ruthless. When we stopped for gas he rolled out two new tires and threw them in the trunk.

"Damn, you're a good stealing nigga," exclaimed JT.

"Hell yeah," I added.

"I know I'm a boss bandit," he countered, "but hey, keep it down baby, keep it down." He gave us a fifth of Jack Daniels and even had a cold Sprite and cups in his pocket.

"You've gotta let us see that coat Sugar," I said admiringly. Even though he had promised to show us some moves (which he didn't), he was very reluctant to let us examine his coat.

"I don't let that many people get close to Sue Belle, they might try to take her from me, then I'd have to cut 'em."

"We ain't even gon' touch her, just let us see inside that bitch," JT promised.

"When we make our stop, I'll think about it," he assured us. When we got back to the city he had JT take him to this old run down lounge where he went in, got some boxes, and came back out. "Ya'll help me take this in so we can get paid," he said as he motioned us out of the car. JT opened the trunk and we made what seemed like a hundred trips. As we pulled away Sugar reached into his coat and pulled out five twenty-dollar bills.

"Here," he said, handing me twenty dollars and giving JT eighty.

"I didn't say I wanted that fag to get none of my money," whined JT.

"Let the brother have something to fold," reasoned Sugar. "He was down with us, that's your boy ain't it?"

"He's my ten dollar boy, not my twenty dollar boy," smiled JT as I made teasing faces at him.

"Stop up the street at that red car," instructed Sugar, "and I'll be right back." JT eased the Impala to the curb and Sugar hopped out.

"Shidd, Bruno needs to permanently take Sugar's spot," remarked JT as he played with his earnings.

"That's easy for you to say," I moaned as I unfolded my tattered twenty.

"Give me that, you don't need it," snarled JT as he playfully tried to snatch my bill.

"You'd better watch out before you draw back a nub goddamit," I warned. "I'm already mad cause I made three dollars an hour." JT cracked up and I had to join him laughing; hell it was pitiful pay for a whole day's work.

Just then Sugar opened the door. "Let's roll Kato." Which reminded me, I had missed the Green Hornet. Now I was really mad. We pulled up in front of this dilapidated old brownstone on forty-third street and Sugar instructed JT to turn the car off.

"I'm just gon' be a minute. Come on, ya'll can go with me." We eagerly bounced out of the car anxious to witness more of Sugar's magic. The snow was crunchy as we entered the downstairs hall that had no glass in the door, a super pissy stench, and not one light bulb to lead us to the squeaky wooden stairs. At the top of the landing Sugar knocked on the door, three quick raps and two short ones.

"Who dat," came a deep voice from within.

"The Sugar man," answered our cleaver guide. The door opened a couple of inches and a big eyeball gave us a thorough inspection before swinging open just wide enough to let us in. We entered an empty foyer with a linoleum floor and once again, no light. Which was no big deal because when you live in the ghetto you're gonna go into a bunch of raggedy cribs with no light bulbs. Lamps were a luxury and people generally had light only in the room where they were. The guy that let us in was a big dude. I couldn't see his features in the dark, but they had sent the right dude to the door that's for damn sure. As we walked down a long hall past an empty living room area I realized we were in a work house, a place where nobody really lived, but just came to cut and package their dope and take care of other low-profile business. The back room was big with long tables along two of the walls like the kind they have in the lunchroom at school. There were old kitchen chairs with the cotton stuffing coming out pushed up to the tables. The windows were all covered up with what seemed to be black plastic garbage bags and duct tape. There was one light in the middle of the ceiling and a funky looking bathroom off to the side with a leaky faucet.

"Who you got with you Sugar," asked the big dude who had let us in."

"I'm breakin' these young brothers in," replied Sugar. "This is Billy, and this is Ray," he said pointing to JT and then me. Me and JT looked at each other and smiled as if to say, "Sugar is too cool, giving us aliases." The fact was, everybody in there was called something other than their names. There was Sugar, the big dude who let us in, a real tall skinny guy in the corner, and two other cats who seemed to be working together. They all gave us the once over and then went about their business. It didn't take long to come to a complete understanding of what was going on. All over the floor were spent matches, matchbooks, and little droplets of blood everywhere. On the table by each man was a package of brown powder and an outfit (a little kit that contained some fashion of a hypodermic needle, a spoon, matches, etc.). We were in a shooting gallery. JT and I looked at each other in realization that we were about to see something that most regular people don't ever see. We grabbed two seats from the far wall and pulled up close to Sugar's spot at the table. We leaned in tight as he pulled out a worn leather pouch that zippered all around and opened it. Me and JT's eyes were riveted on Sugar's every move. He was showing us some art now and this day would prove to be one I'd never forget. Sugar stopped and looked us both square in the eyes. I thought he was gonna offer us a shot

"O.K., who you see here, and what you see here, stays right up in here, right?" "Oh hell yeah, no doubt," we answered in earnest.

"All right, I don't want no shit," scolded Sugar.

"Naw man, we cool," reassured JT. I nodded in agreement. Inside Sugar's pouch was a tiny little spoon that looked like antique silver, and was very cool. There was a book of matches and a long plastic case such that a thermometer might come in. He pulled a small aluminum foil package out of his pocket and laid it on the table. At that moment he could have pulled a jet engine out of that coat and we wouldn't have been surprised. He gently unfolded the foil exposing some brown powder which I knew to be heroin (I'd been around it enough at Woodrow's to identify it by smell). He gently shook a portion of it into the spoon and sat it down, then he broke off a match, lit it, and slowly ran it under the spoon cooking the dope. JT and I leaned in so close that Sugar said, "Goddamn, can my dope breathe please?" We snickered covering our mouths so as not to disturb his package and get our asses kicked and moved back, only inches.   When the powder was completely melted it looked like a spoonful of clear, golden cod liver oil with brown bubbles around the edges. We could see the silver spoon through the liquid. We were mesmerized. Every move Sugar made we followed like little chicken hawks. The building could have fallen down around us and we wouldn't have known it. He very carefully placed the spoon on the table with the short handle resting on his pouch so that none of the precious juice would spill. Then he then lifted the long plastic container from the pouch. Inside was an eyedropper with a needle secured at the open end with a mini rubber band. The needle was real tiny and as he gently blew it, I suppose to knock off any dust that may have settled there, he looked at each of us and gave a confident wink. We smiled as he depressed the dropper end of the outfit and drew the liquid up. He turned it upside down with the needle facing the ceiling and popped it a coupla times with a gentle flicking of his finger. This was to make any air bubbles inside rise to the top. He then sat the spike gingerly on the table with the needle end slightly elevated on the pouch. He stood up, removed his coat (which he neatly folded), took off his belt and rolled up his sleeve. At that moment I just happened to look around the room and to my wonderment, every man was similarly engaged. It was like a ballet and the dope melting, coat-folding portion of the program had just ended. It was amazing how each man was self contained and intent in his individual order of business and yet, they were the essence of synchronism. It's funny how meticulous a dope fiend can be. They all had their outfits neatly housed in some sort of tidy little package. None of their coats were haphazardly strewn across a chair, and they were all moving very methodically with no wasted effort. Sugar rolled up his sleeve, wrapped his belt around his arm, and pulled it tight with his teeth. His skin looked terrible, as though someone had used steel wool to scrape up and down his arm leaving little scabs all over it. As he pulled the belt tight he smacked his inner arm trying to raise a vein. He searched and searched and when he found a suitable spot, reached over, grabbed the spike and flicked it with his fingers as he held it to the light. He then squeezed the dropper until there was a tiny globule of liquid at the tip and very slowly eased it onto his arm, under the skin, and into the vein. My brow was furrowed as I watched the liquid slowly move through the dropper about half way and then stop. His fingers released pressure on the dropper and the subsequent vacuum created in the spike caused blood to back up into it, eerily mixing with the golden dope looking like a Lava Lamp in a process known as 'jacking off.' He let go of the dropper as the concoction did its mystic dance inside the clear plastic spike. Sugar's eyes rolled back, his head lolled, and his jaw dropped open as a delirious shudder of ecstasy rumbled through his body. Saliva ran down the belt end still dangling precariously in his mouth. He released a pent-up exhalation as his whole body relaxed into a deep nod. At that moment I heard the thunderous ticking of my wristwatch and realized the room was perfectly still. JT was engrossed in the needle stuck in Sugar's arm. We watched blood ooze from the puncture, down the spike, and onto the floor. I slowly turned to take in the rest of the room and every man was lost in a deep nod. Some had their heads on their chests while others were swayed back with their mouths wide open, eyes rolled back, spikes hanging, and blood silently dripping onto the floor. With our jaws dropped and our hearts pounding, JT and I didn't make a sound as we slowly surveyed this grim pageant of ghetto misery. These were our men, our black men pirouetting in the opera of dangling death. There they were in suspended animation somewhere between purgatory and hell in a black hole from which there was no escape. Just then one of the men sitting closest to Sugar began to sway his leg from side to side while rolling his head from his chest to the hanging back position. Sugar sniffed and another exhaled as they all seemed to come out of their nods at the same time, not unlike one of those sci-fi movies where astronauts put to sleep on a long space journey all wake up together. Sugar looked at us through a drowsy humor as if to acknowledge our presence and make sure we hadn't touched his stuff. The belt had fallen out of his mouth, but not to the point where it had knocked the spike from his arm. He simply removed the belt and slowly shot the remaining juice into his vein. This time he emitted a dragging moan but kept his eyes open.

"Oh shit, I feel good baby," Sugar drawled.

"Me too," moaned the big cat who'd let us in.

Sugar carefully plucked the spike from his vein, wiped the trail of blood from his arm, struggled to his feet, and stumbled into the bathroom. "Goddamn ye apothecary thy drugs are quick!" shouted Sugar, as the room erupted into peals of laughter and verbal affirmations all around. As if by magic the room was transformed from a morgue into a party, just like that.

"Come on Sugar, get out of the bathroom so I can wash my jack," bellowed one of the guys.

Sugar shouted from the bathroom, "O.k. baby, o.k., let the sweet man get his shit together."

"Shidd, the sweet man got his shit together already today, I can tell," testified another.

"Hell yeah," affirmed big man, "that nigga can steal the meat out of a weenie without touchin' the skin."

"You got that right," added the tall skinny cat.

"Look here goddamit," protested Sugar as he swaggered from the bathroom, "I know I'm a boss bandit of the first rank, but you ain't got to put my business in the street." "Yo business *is* the street nigga," said another, and on it went. This was as lively a bunch of crooks as I'd ever seen. The banter went on as Sugar packed up his goods, zipped his pouch, and grabbed his coat.

"Yo Sugar," squeaked JT, "you gon' let us check out Sue Belle like you said?"

"Yeah," bellowed big man, "Show us that monstrosity."

Sugar looked at JT as he swung into his coat. "See, you had a chance til you got all these crooks checkin' my game, now I'm gon' have to lock her up."

Just then one of the guys in the back came over. "Yo shorty, don't believe that shit, he never let nobody peep that rag." JT and I just laughed, because we believed him.

Sugar reached into his pocket and pulled out a pint of Canadian Club. "Here goddamit wet your thozzels," as he handed them the bottle, "big man, catch the door!" As we walked out the other fellas could only shake their heads in amazement at the dept of Sugar's pockets.

"Later Sugar," they shouted as big man let us out.

"Adios muchachos," saluted Sugar as the door closed behind us. All day Sugar had been in keen spirits, but now he was hoppin', finger poppin', and be-boppin'. He whistled a little tune as he bobbed his head in rhythm from side to side.

"Drop me off on the tre-nine JT," he said in the smoothest street drawl I'd ever heard, "and remember, today is quiet as kept."

"No doubt," said JT as the Impala lurched away from the curb. "No doubt."

WOODROW TAKIN' OVER

JoJo was a straight-up dope fiend who didn't know who he was half the time. Bruno was a dope fiend leg breaker who eventually got himself shot to pieces by some Latino drug boys over on the west side. Woodrow's mother never had anything to do with the business side of the operation, and his sister only spent the money, she never had to worry about any of it. So when Papa D fell on some icy steps and busted a few ribs it was Woodrow he called to the hospital to give detailed take over instructions should he take a turn for the worse. Woodrow was still in high school but he was sensible, fair, and well liked in the neighborhood. He'd be an excellent successor to the throne however, that wasn't going to be necessary because all Papa D had was a few broken ribs. That's what we thought. Papa D was a chain smoker and kept a bottle of Crown Royal by his side at all times. There were complications. Infection had set up in his lungs and his heart was having a hard time handling the stress. The whole neighborhood was stunned, holding its collective breath not unlike a nation when its leader is stricken. His enemies were positioning themselves strategically while his soldiers scurried about in hushed tones as if a war council was being convened. Woodrow, while acting like a leader, was visibly shaken. He ordered all of Papa D's debts paid in full immediately. Jo Jo had to assume Bruno's old job as leg breaker and a lot of people got shook down. I guess Woodrow figured there were those who might try to play dumb with their debts if the ole' man died, and that wouldn't be good for business. Wood needed his boys now more than ever before. We worked the doors, counted money, and made sure every gram of dope was accounted for. For the first time Woodrow's sister who normally got wads of money from Papa D had to go through channels.

Then it happened. Papa D died. There has never been or ever will be a funeral service like Papa D's. Every pimp, hustler, prostitute, dope fiend, housewife, mechanic, man, woman, and child on the South Side of Chicago showed up to pay their respects. It was the most unbelievable outpouring of love for one man I had ever seen. Even Smiley who ran all the territory North of thirty-fifth street showed up.

"Yo little D, I just want to say that I'm sorry about your loss. Your Papa was a good man. We had our differences because of our business so they weren't gonna go away, but even when we were in jail and some things went down he never brought it street side. He was smart the way he handled things."

Woodrow extended his hand to the man whose name was dirt in the jects. "I appreciate that Smiley and I want you to know that my daddy never said nothin' bad about you, so as far as I'm concerned there ain't no truck between us as long as things stay the way they are."

Smiley clasped both of his hands around Wood's. "You got the same mellow way like yo' daddy. Everything is cool, and I hope the next time we meet it won't be under such sad circumstances."

"All right now Smiley" said Woodrow, "you be cool." Most of the night was just that way, but not all of it. Another cat named Weasel came to pay his respects and didn't get such a warm reception.

"How you doin little brother," whined the nasal talking Weasel.

"I'm okay. Long time no see," returned Woodrow. "Yeah, I just got out of the County when I heard about your old man. Damn, that's a shame." Just then JoJo stepped up.

"Well if ain't the Weasel."

"Uh, hey JoJo, how you be man?" stammered the now very nervous Weasel. JoJo got right in Weasel's face.

"I'm surprised to see you up in here. You know there's been talk about you and them Latin Kings or should I say now Disciples over on the west side."

"What you mean man?" Weasel was visibly sweating.

"I ain't got nothin' to do with them boys."

"That ain't what we heard," growled JoJo getting even closer to the Weasel.

147

"Word is you had something to do with my brother gettin' popped." I thought the Weasel would have a heart attack right there.

"Aw man come on, don't lay that on me man. Me and Bruno wuz cool. I swear on the eyes of my son I'm loyal to ya'll man."

Just then Woodrow's mother stepped between JoJo and the Weasel. "This is your father's wake, need I say more?"

Several of JoJo's soldiers were right there ready to take the Weasel outside to meet the truth, but Woodrow said, "go up and pay your respects Weasel then get lost, forever." That must have been pretty nerve wracking for the Weasel because I could tell he was afraid to leave the funeral parlor. He was probably thinking the boys would follow him out and make it official. He eventually slipped off and sure enough, I never saw him again.

Woodrow was now the man, and although he learned well from Papa D, he ran a different house. "The old man was too soft on muh fuckas," I remember him saying,

"I ain't havin' that shit. If somebody wants to borrow money, they gon' hafta pay." And that's the way it was. He began squeezing dope fiends on merchandise they brought to the house and he didn't forgive the soldiers with a pat on the back when they occasionally came up short the way Papa D did. But what I thought was truly his undoing, was that he didn't treat the elder mothers the way the Ole' Man did. There had been a lot of talk going around the jects about how nobody had gotten Thanksgiving baskets, so JT asked him about it.

"You didn't give out Thanksgiving turkeys, what's up with that?"

"I just forgot man, that's all," was Woodrow's answer.

"How did you forget something like that?"

"I've got a lot of shit on my mind man, things I never had to think about before. I can't keep up with all that bullshit."

"That ain't bullshit man, those are your people out there. This is your livelihood. They're the ones that keep yo' ass in business; you fuckin up."

"I never asked to do this shit JT. This shit was thrown on me. If my brothers had any sense they'd be here instead of me. I don't want to do this shit, I want to go back to the beach, I want to run some hoes, fuck them muh fuckas!" Woodrow had tears in his eyes and right then I saw a young boy's life in the fell clutch of circumstance. In his eyes I saw every kid that lived in these projects, happy and free until the dilemma of their existence became glaringly evident; when we all had to make that blindly inconceivable choice to give up or fight. To take that wide heavily traveled road to drugs, jail time, and death, or choose the narrow rocky road to hope for a bright future. I'd never felt sorry for Woodrow before because it seemed he'd had everything a boy could want, but I felt sorry for him now. I knew things were going sideways when he started spending a lot of money. He bought his sister a new car, he bought his mother a house in Cleveland, and he bought himself a brownstone on Forty Seventh Street. Woodrow wasn't the prince anymore, he was something else, but then, we all were.

WOOD . . . THE MAN

Woodrow hated selling dope. He was a kid for crying out loud. He wanted to be outside from sun-up to sundown running in only for Kool-Aid and stuff. The stuff being his baseball glove or bat. Notice I said glove not mitt. White boys played with mitts, we played with gloves. He'd run in and get some money for ice cream if we all were running home to beg for ice cream money. Wood ran in to "get" some money, not beg. Or he'd go and snatch his mini-bike out of the kitchen when we were all going for a quick ride. Me, JT, and Woodrow had mini-bikes. We worked one Summer when we were fourteen and bought them.

Back in the early seventies in summertime Chicago, the city employed thousands of young kids to keep 'em off the streets and doing wrong things. They'd be goofy kinds of jobs like picking up paper off the streets all day long. It was kind of a trip because you'd be picking up paper and stuff that you remembered throwing onto the ground the night before, and getting paid for it! Or if you were lucky you'd get a job in one of the neighborhood park's field houses as like some sort of counselor for day camp kids. All you did really was play games and eat free lunches.

In the Summers there was free food up the ying yang: choke sandwiches that came with free milk or juice, thick government cheese that every household in the projects had, and even full course TV dinner style meals that adults came to scarf down in the early evenings. We nick-named our neighborhood field house the 'Hungry House' because every hungry project dweller, dope fiend, wine head, pimps with all their hoes, and even families (like ours) would line up to eat. There was so much government cheese that we used to throw it at each other in cheese fights. You wouldn't think that getting hit with a chunk of cheese was any big deal, but I'm here to tell you, turn your face into a Dino powered cheese-chunk and yo ass was going home. It was wonderland I tell ya, and nobody who wanted to work went without a job. You really didn't have to worry about the dope fiends and wine heads fouling up the works because it was minimum wage and payday was every two weeks. That simply wouldn't do for an individual who had to get it on everyday. So it was pretty much only school kids working (if you can call it that) all over the city. And that's what city policy makers had in mind I guess. Anyway, me, JT, and Woodrow took one of those two-week checks and bought mini bikes from Steinmart for $114.00 each. We were out of control maniacs after that. Buzzing up and down the sidewalks, in the streets, or pulled over talking to girls. Oh Man it was a blast! Who would want to go up stairs and sell dope through the gate on their front door? Wood was just a kid.

MOMMY DEAREST

As project mothers go I have to admit we had a good one. My Mother wasn't loud, drunk, or abusive. Even on welfare she was an excellent provider. We always had toys at Christmas and little parties on our birthdays. I should mention here that my mother was pretty and after she got rid of my father once and for all she never had a problem getting a boyfriend who helped her support her kids. It's interesting how your parents being your primary teachers completely shape everything you are. My Mom's parents taught her how to be selfish and at an early age we were taught that we didn't have to care so much about each other as we did for ourselves. Observing my mother's cavalcade of boyfriends (who had to be paying) cheapened my sense of loyalty to the opposite sex and emphasized instead what I could get out of them. Then she met Tick. He was a tall, slick talking, hype (heroin user for the hip impaired) who came in and injected our crib with pure adrenalin. It took a while for me to understand that his hour-long forays into the bathroom were actually shoot-up sessions that of course took time. He had to fire the drugs, shoot the drugs, jack the drugs, nod then wake up, clean up, and come out poppin'. This process couldn't be hurried so he made an announcement beforehand that if anyone wanted to use the bathroom they'd best be getting with it. Oh did I mention that in order to maintain a drug habit you had to be a good thief (ala Sugar). Tick was a master and he taught moms the craft. It started with meats. Us kids would accompany her to Jewels where we would block the action by standing around the cart acting like we were examining cereal (or some other big boxed blocking aid) while she stuffed a roast in her purse. This is very important because this is where we learned the "Booster's Face." That's the benign look on a thief's face that throws off store personnel and onlookers . . . totally innocent. Learning that as a young kid is essential to your development as a boss bandit. We then graduated to K Mart, Sears, and other department stores where we'd put on new shoes and leave our old ones on the rack. I remember once we were leaving K Mart wearing new shoes when the store dicks stopped us and marched my moms and all three of our little asses to the back where they had our old raggedy shoes on a table. They let us go with a warning never to come back.

We didn't. We went to the mall instead with a band of other boosting broads and their kids. I remember many trips to Evergreen Plaza with two or three cars full of kids and slick mamas ready to heist. They'd leave us in the parking lot and go in for about an hour or so of uninterrupted spree glee. Then they'd come out all heavily laden with merch, hop in the car, and hightail it back to one of their cribs. Then the trading, bickering, straight-up fighting began.

"Girl, you know I wanted that green blouse to go with these pants."

"Well you should've got 'em then bitch."

"Who you callin a bitch?"

"If the shoe fits . . . which reminds me, give me then damn black shoes!"

Mayhem.

I learned early on there is no honor among thieves. We had a good mama and she provided for us. She made sure we had a clean shot at a quality education, and carved out what I thought was some decent emotional stability for my siblings and me.

What I would realize many years later is that she taught us how to be selfish, how to lie, steal, and be completely dysfunctional when it came to relationships. Or perhaps she equipped us to go out there ready for a cruel world. Maybe I just misused the tools.

SECOND STORY LAMONT

So now I'd found my diversion, stealing and girls. Stealing was a part of my up bringing. My mother justified it all as a necessity of survival.

"We're just doin' what we have to do," she'd say.

I was convinced that everybody did it so it wasn't a big deal.

The high school I went to wasn't in the projects and most of the kids there lived in homes all over the city. I remember going to a school friend's house with two bottles of Wild Irish Rose Wine one night only to find no one home. I don't know where the impulse came from but the next thing I knew I was climbing through the second floor window. There was a stereo, two T.V.'s, and a couple of nice clocks that I quickly hauled out to my mother's car. I'll never forget her reaction when she opened the door and saw me heavily laden with stereo equipment. She stuck her head out the door, looked both ways and said,   "Boy, get in here!" After that I was breaking into cribs all the time. Any neighbors I didn't like, got hit. Third floor, fourth floor, it didn't matter I was a cat. Even Woodrow was surprised.

"Man where you gettin' all these T.V.'s?"

"Damn where I'm gettin' em, just don't be giving me no short trap for this good stuff."

"You get a third like everybody else goddamit, you stealin' like everybody else!"

"I'm your boy though. I need to get a bonus or something," I said incredulously.   "You can bonus yo' ass away from here and get me one of those new microwave ovens." I hadn't seen one of those microwaves in anybody's house because they were new, big, and expensive.

"I'm Al Monday goddamit, if I can't get it, then it can't be got." Al Monday was the name of a television character on a show called, 'It Takes A Thief.'

"Well get your ass out there Al and hook me up," goaded Woodrow. Needless to say he got his microwave. I had to bust in a school to get it.

I was still lifeguarding every summer, only now I was working at Fuller Park Pool. There were plenty of girls over there and I was having a ball.

"You the new lifeguard?" was the way the honeys would cut into me.

"I'm the new HEAD lifeguard, what's your name?" That's the way it went. They'd hang around all day and by the evening I'd have them in the pool playing with them, swimming through their legs, and teaching them how to swim with my hands full of titties. I hooked up a mattress in the boiler room and once again it was on.

Since I was the elder guard all the honeys had to come through me, and looking back, the younger guards never complained about my honorarium because I was showing 'em the ropes. They bought me cakes on my birthday and always came and got me whenever there was a fine chick anywhere in the park; for instruction. They were in genuine awe of me and considered themselves with it to have a real player style mack daddy at their pool. I bought a car, a motorcycle, and sold a little weed from time to time. My brother and sister thought I was a god, my mother called me her 'Number one son' because I was still going to school everyday and making some decent grades. I liked school. I used to bring girls home during the day while my mother was at job training and do the wild thang. I boned 'em in my car (which by the way was a station wagon), made clothes in tailoring shop, and even had my hair finger-waved at one point. I was so full of myself nobody could tell me shit. Then the bottom fell out.

ALL THAT GLITTERS

That day at the shooting gallery played in my mind long after Sugar got out of the car. How could it not? I'd never seen anything like that before or since. The red dots were banging around in my head like pinballs in an arcade game. I was transfixed on the needle in the golden dope as the magical elixir traveled up into the makeshift hypodermic. I squinted as its razor sharp point pierced the scaly skin and began the magical transformation from man to mystical marionette. I was endowed with x-ray vision as I followed it through the vein and into the heart where it was hydraulically speed pumped to the brain resulting in instantaneous euphoria. I wanted to fire some drugs so bad I didn't know what to do.

There was a lifeguard who worked with me at Fuller Park named Hercules. They called him "Herc" for short. Now that I think about it, I'm sure his real name wasn't Hercules, but I never saw his pay stub. It's a trip because he was this real strong muscle dude see, and If that was his real name, how could his parents have known when he was born that Hercules would be perfect for him? Anyway, he was a hype and one day he came to me drug sick as hell begging for ten dollars.

"C'mon Lamont, I'm sick as shit and I really, really, really need a hit." All I had was twenty dollars and I wasn't about to give it to this fool.

"Man, I ain't got it."

He came right back with, "C'mon man I know you got ten dollars. Can you stand a search?" There, he'd said it, the phrase that for every project kid meant you done stopped playing and went semi-serious.

"All right man, I've got twenty dollars but I need it to get lunch for the rest of the week. Plus I've got to put some gas in my motorcycle. I can't do it Herc."

"You can give me half man," he pleaded, as his body suddenly seemed closer to me than before.

Okay, let's assess the situation: we're in the locker room alone. Herc outweighs me by ninety pounds, easy. AND he's a dope sick heroin addict who KNOWS where twenty dollars is.

I got real sympathetic but not forceful. "Look man I know where you are right now but you know we don't get paid until Friday and how am I gonna get to work with no gas?" His eyes bored into the marrow of my bones with a directness.

"Lamont, I'm gonna fuckin die right here if I don't get right."

From deep in my subconscious where Freudian thoughts, wishes, and curiosities dwell just waiting to pop out came, " Aight, you asked for ten dollars, I got twenty. I'll give you the whole nut if you'll come back and do me." Crickets.

Time stood still as if every clock in the world, every car, every boiling pot and baby crying stopped. I saw a bead of sweat roll down from Herc's cowlick to his temple, his cheekbone, and finally silently drop from his chin.

"Okay," came his weak, shocked, disappointed reply. His eyes filled with incredulity and pain, guilt and defeat. I'd stung him. This monster of a man already crumbling, succumbed to the final hammer's blow, and with a deep sigh . . . "okay."

"I ain't bullshittin," I cautioned before pulling the bill all the way out. "I want the shit so come back and do me . . . just a little." He averted his eyes and took the bill ashamedly as he turned away.

"Aight," he sputtered, "I'll be right back."

While he was gone, I paced the locker room floor slapping the veins in my inner arm, working my scared-to-death nerves up, imagining the position I wanted to be in when the rush cascaded through my body blotting out all reality. I slumped against the lockers and slid down to the floor.

"Oh my god, this is it!"

I didn't see Herc for two weeks . . . bastard.

DINO - STICK UP KID

Dino was looking all over for Duh Duh. He hunted us down at Woodrow's brownstone where we were hanging out getting zooted (getting high, for . . .you know) watching a basketball game.

"Woodrow, go down and see who's laying on your doorbell like that," JT hollered down the long hall leading to the kitchen.

"Whoever it is 'bout to get his ass kicked, I know that," shouted Woodrow coming from the back of the house.

"That's Dino's dumb ass," he snarled as he pulled back the living room curtains. "What that fool want?" After unlocking the one hundred dead bolts on the door Dino was finally in.

"Ya'll must be deaf, I been out there ten minutes," puffed Dino breathing hard. "Yall seen Duh Duh?"

"Now you know Duh Duh up on the north side bonin' that hoe," said JT

"Or gettin' boned," added Woodrow. We all cracked up.

"You know you wrong Wood," Dino cautioned barely able to hold back his laughter. "Just because her hands is all big and she's got a big back ain't no reason to dog your boy."

"Man you see them dukes?" countered Wood. "Looks like she could knock out Ali."

I couldn't hold back any longer. "If that bitch does have a dick, then what the fuck is Duh Duh doing?" I questioned playfully cocking my head to the side.

JT just shook his head. "Raimy Boy told me he's been buying up all the acid he can get his hands on."

"Trippin' with a trick, goddamn!" Wood wouldn't let up and we all found ourselves rolling with laughter once again at Duh Duh's expense. Dino brought us back to earth temporarily.

"Look man I need to find him right now."

"So what's the scoop Dino?" asked JT, "ya'll gon stick up some more crap games?"

"That's not what we call it, we call it fighting crime," corrected Dino.

"How you fighting crime pullin' out a gun goddamit?" asked Woodrow. "They know gambling is illegal hell, if they weren't breakin' the law maybe they'd get to keep their money."

I kinda figured I knew what Dino's answer would be but I just had to ask. "Dino what happened to your dream of being a pro athlete?" He let out this big sigh as if he was tired of answering the same question over and over; but honestly, I think it was him who had been asking it.

"They ain't lettin' me do my thing man. They got it hooked up so that only the white boys and a few brainy brothers with good grades can play. What pro team cares if I can't read and write, as long as I can run that ball? They don't. It's the white man that don't want us makin' all that money and dominatin' their sports! I can out run everybody in that school but they got it fixed up to be hard so a lot of us don't make it. That's what happened to my goddamn dream!" He was raging and there wasn't anything we could say. "So if they want to keep me from runnin' on the field then I'll run on the streets. They still can't catch me!" I was sorry I had asked, and from the looks on everybody's faces, the feeling was unanimous.

"I don't know how to get in touch with Duh Duh," whispered JT.

"That's aight, mo' for me." Dino pulled out the gun I'd sold him, flipped open the cylinder, checked his bullets, and headed for the door.

"Dino," Woodrow shouted as the door slammed shut with thunderous concussion.

That was the last time we'd see Dino alive.

That night he tried to stick up a crap game, and while he had the drop on some of the dudes takin' their money, a cat behind him pulled out a pistol and shot him in the head.   They took his gym shoes.

Ever since he was a kid Dino kept a nice clean pair of gym shoes. He said athletes needed to have "good rubber on their feet at all times," I guess he was right, they didn't want him to make it.

IT COULD BE WORSE . . . IT COULD BE RAINING

"So what's your name again?"

"Linda . . . Linda Oasis" she replied brightly.

For a split second Duh Duh almost gave her the "Duh" look he was famous for. "Linda OASIS, that's your REAL name?"

"Yes," she said indignantly with a little neck roll.

"That's the name on your birth certificate?" asked Duh Duh as if looking over the rim of imaginary glasses.

"I should know my own name," she said flatly, with the look of someone tired of being asked the same thing over and over.

Duh Duh sensing he was losing her quickly recovered. "Damn, that shit is hot!"
"Thank you," came the flattered response with batting eyelashes; now he was back on track.

"And so are you, if I must say-so myself," giving her the up and down.

"You can say it," she countered.

Duh Duh had never gotten this far with any girl one-on-one rapping, so he was in unchartered waters, but not drowning, he was feeling it...not drowning. And plus he was clean. Him and Dino had been hittin licks all over town and he was decked out in his fresh new walking suit that he'd had made to match his new burnt orange Bally Gators. He also had a burnt orange Kangol pimp cocked on his head, homeboy was definitely clean.

"Soooooo, you live around here or what, I ain't never seen you before."

"I was over my cousin's house down on Calumet, but then her Boyfriend came by and I started feeling like three was a crowd, you know? So I was 'bout to get in my car and head out when I heard the Spinners playing down here, and that's my jam!"

Record stores in the hood would play whatever 45 you wanted to hear so you could be sure it was what you wanted. They had speakers outside the store, usually over the door so the whole street was treated to tantalizing hits all day long. She'd heard "'Could It Be I'm Falling In Love," and sure enough had come in with her dollar to buy it.

From seemingly out of nowhere at every turn Duh Duh was in rare form. "Damn, your cousin was right on time," he spit out as smooth as silk. Linda laughed and put her hand on his shoulder sending heat waves straight to his pubes.

"You say you wuz about to get in your car, what kinda car you got?"

"A Deuce and a Quarter." The silky words rolling off her tongue as if she'd practiced saying them in the mirror for hours. You see, in 1975 Big City USA, the Buick Electra 225 (with 225 affectionately referred to as Deuce and a Quarter) was THE pimp car to have after the Cadillac Eldorado. If somebody said they were pushing a Deuce, they were instantly elevated to premiere status.

"A Deuce?" Duh Duh's face transformed into incredulous worship.

"You know it," she said jauntily. Damn, she was fine as hell and cocky too. Them tight bell-bottoms were hugging her ass as if they were painted on. She had on one of them little silky blouses that was tied at the waist revealing a perfect navel and breasts that looked so soft and plump that if she loosened one more button he'd just have to sink his face right in 'em.

"You got a Deuce and a Quarter?" (just one more time please just in case his hearing wasn't right)

"You wanna see it?"

Duh Duh was completely oblivious to whatever record was playing at the time. He forgot all about Dino and him being a tag-along flunky with a low IQ. He had been transformed into Willy Dynamite and this chick was Cleopatra Jones. "I don't just want to see it, I wonts to get up in it!"

Linda Oasis gave him the sultry once over, bit her bottom lip, and in the sexiest voice ever uttered by a human being said, "That can be arranged."

THINGS FALL APART

Dino's funeral was real sad because we all felt like we should've done something. His mother, brothers, and sisters were all glad to see us, yet there was an eerie sense of steely-eyed detachment. Maybe it was our guilt, or maybe they somehow blamed us for Dino's death, or not being there to prevent it.

"Ya'll gon' need some help," Dino's mother managed to utter through the reddest eyes I've ever seen.

"Ma'am?" questioned JT

"There's only four of ya'll and it takes six to carry a casket."

Then she broke down so bad I swear I wished I was somewhere else. Dino's older brother and two of his sisters ran over and helped JT and Woodrow carry her over to a pew.

"Who else gon' help us carry Dino?" asked Duh Duh.

"Gino and Pritchard Hicks," I told him. Gino was Dino's older brother. He had never touched a drug in his life. He wanted to be a policeman and he said they drug tested so he couldn't get high. We used to laugh and call him Officer Friendly. No one was laughing now.

It seemed like every time we hung out after that somebody would say something that would make us think of Dino. It was a bummer. So without any announcements or anything, everybody sorta started doing their own thing. That winter me and Stevie D., who was in my tailoring class, started going to a lot of clubs and sweet-talking a lot of girls. Woodrow concentrated on his business, and Duh Duh disappeared. Word was, he'd run up quite a credit debt with Woodrow on a bunch of pills and Woodie was lookin' to get squared up. Nobody knew what JT was doing. On New Year's Eve we always partied at Woodrow's crib, but this year Duh Duh and JT weren't there, and of course Dino.

"Where the hell is JT and Duh Duh?" I asked Wood.

"I know one thing, Duh Duh better have a pocket full of money when he do show up or we gon' fight."

"Nigga, Duh Duh's cockstrong ass will kill you," I jabbed trying to lighten the conversation.

"Fool is you crazy?" defended Woodrow indignantly. "That punk so doped up and weak in the knees by that dick-licka it wouldn't even be fair."

"And JT." He pulled me over to the wall because he was about to mention a name that would perk up ears if other people in the house heard it. "You know JT hangin' with Sugar."

"He hustling with Sugar?" I asked flatly.

"I don't know what they doin but JT been pickin' him up off his post for the last coupla' months."

"When, after he gets off work?" I asked.

"I think so, 'cause a lot of times he still has on his Post Office uniform."

"What! I know JT ain't goin' out poppin' with his uniform on!" I said unable to believe my ears.

"Whatever they're doin'," said Woodrow, "it must be mighty damn good, 'cause JT ain't comin' upstairs...he ain't even gettin' out of the car." Now I'm wondering if JT is makin' moves with Sugar and cuttin' his road dog out of the action.

"Uh huh," was all I could say, "uh huh."

January first I was at JT's mother's door. I didn't see his car, but I knew sometimes he'd park on the other side of Madden Park pool if he didn't want anyone to know he was there.

"How you doing Ms. tate. Is JT home?"

"Hey Lamont. Naw, Jerome ain't here right now, he's somewhere with Sugar." My face nearly fell to the floor but I somehow managed to pick it up, and put it back on before she noticed.

"You know Sugar?" I managed to stammer.

"Well, I never met him, but I know they work together at the Post Office." I was damn near speechless.

"Uh huh."

"And that they bowl on the Post Office bowling team." As she spoke I almost bust out laughing at the stretch JT had laid on her. "They usually just bowl on Wednesday, Friday, and Saturday, but since they've got this big tournament coming up they been practicing every night for the last three weeks."

"Oh yeah, that's right." I managed some feigned semblance of discovery.

"I didn't think they'd be practicin' on New Years, but you know Jerome, he does things all the way," she said beaming with pride.

"Yes ma'am," I said, knowing only too well. "If he calls tell him I stopped by."

"Alright then, you be good."

"Yes ma'am."

As the snow crunched under the new penny loafers I'd gotten for Christmas, my mind pictured all the things JT and Sugar could be doing: hittin' railroad cars, liquor stores, equipment warehouses, tractor trailer trucks, goddamn! I was too agitated to stay in the house so I went up to see Woodrow. He wasn't there so I figured he was at his brownstone and headed on over. As I neared Forty-Seventh I was in such deep thought that I nearly missed JT's car parked in the cut on Forty-third street.

"Damn that looked like JT's ride," I said aloud as I tipped over for a closer look. When I got to Forty-third street I suddenly recognized the building as the one Sugar had taken me and JT to that night to fire them drugs. "Well I'll be goddamned," I said as I approached JT's unmistakable Blue Impala with the doughnut tires. "That mutha fucka."

THE BOILING FROG

"If a frog is put suddenly into boiling water, it will jump out, but if the frog is put in cold water which is then brought to a boil slowly, it will not perceive the danger and will be cooked to death."

Linda Oasis started out cool then slowly turned up the heat. Her titties were always bursting out of her blouse like hot cupcakes rising in the oven. They were gorgeous and he couldn't keep his eyes off of them, but no touching!

"Come on now Ray, we just friends right," she'd admonish when he'd pull her to him bouncing those bad boys off his chest.

"Friends hug don't they?" he pleaded.

"Just so you don't go getting any bright ideas."

Little did she know, Duh Duh never had a bright idea in his life.

She was hot, and Duh Duh had never seen so many varieties of tight little shorts, jean skirts, and flimsy sun dresses in his life . Linda made sure she teased him to the brink of insanity on a daily before giving him his first real kiss. They were parked at 31st Street Beach with a bottle of Gallo White Port and some powdered lemonade Kool-Aid in the 10-cent pack. The operation was that you poured off some of the White Port (chilled as cold as you could get it), poured in the Kool-Aid, shake it vigorously, and wa-la, school boy scotch!

It was dusk on a beautiful Chicago Summer evening, Summer Madness was playing on the radio, and a sweet gentle breeze was blowing ever so lightly. Duh Duh, emboldened by a half bottle of Willie P and an ache in his loins that couldn't be put off any longer turned Linda's face toward his with an ever so gentle nudge of his hand.

"You know how I feel about you Linda, you're more than my friend, you're everything to me." Linda, who was similarly mellow was caught up in the picturesque beauty of the moment and stayed locked in eye to eye with suddenly suave Duh Duh.

"Damn Ray I'm feeling you too. I just don't want to get hurt." Duh Duh had taken control. The moment was his, and her sweet mouth inches from his parted ever so gently.

"I love you girl," were the last words she heard before the rolling sea of emotion cascaded into an exploding crescendo of passion as their tongues gently danced before crashing into one another in a frenzy of ecstasy.

Duh Duh's manhood detonated like fireworks on the fourth of July, and while he was still shuddering her smiling eyes gently opened.

"Aw Baby, that's just what I wanted to do, kiss me again." At once his panic turned into caveman and he not only kissed her savagely, he shoved his hand into her blouse and lustfully caressed her firm, heaving breast. His first kiss, his first nutt, his first lobotomy.

After that Duh Duh's hustling took on a whole different urgency. What was a sport now became must see TV. He needed that money because Linda he discovered liked to get high, and if he was ever going to score from third he'd have to come in with the big guns. He'd been close on several occasions. Once he'd gotten her really hot and tried slipping his hand down her panties. Just as he felt the welcoming tangle of pubic glory she grabbed his hand and pulled it out.

"Come on baby that's special, how about I taste him?"

He couldn't be hearing what he thought he'd heard.

"What do you mean? Your mouth?"

"Good girls don't do the other thing like that," she said. "Oral doesn't really count."

And so it went through June, July, August, September, and October 12th, Duh Duh's birthday. Through summer between them they had smoked nearly a quarter pound of weed, drank gallons of Willy P, snorted boy (heroin), girl (cocaine), dropped Quaaludes, you name it. But their favorite drug, the thing Duh Duh had made more trips to the projects for than anything else, was acid; Purple Microdot, Purple Haze, and Windowpane, the acetylene torch that had their asses so burnt up it's a wonder they could still think straight. And every night when they were tweaked to oblivion, Linda's blowjob would catapult Duh Duh into the cosmos . . . a short hop actually. Linda was the glory hole he'd searched for all his life. And to think, she never gave up the twat until October 12th, Duh Duh's birthday.

"Naw Baby not tonight," evoked Duh Duh. "Tonight you've got to fuck me, you gotta fuck me good. It's my birthday. I need that pussy."

Linda, as if she'd taken the twelve step oath of sobriety sat up and looked deep into Duh Duh's soul. "Do you love me Ray?"

Duh Duh and his dick straightened up and got equally as serious. "I worship you Linda."

"Suppose it's not what you expect," she said innocently.

"I want to marry you." There, he'd said the one thing to which there was no rebuttal; the one thing that un-furrowed her brow.

"No matter what?" she asked slightly biting her lower lip in the most irresistible manner known to man.

"No matter what." Duh Duh's eyes were cloudy and glazed over from way too much acid and Linda's pupils were banging from side to side in their watery sockets. They were fried.

"I'm going to let you hit it from the back, okay?"

"Please, please, please," was all Duh Duh could get out of his mouth. She looked through his pupils, deep into his soul.

"Turn off the lights," she said.

FIGHT OR FLIGHT

I don't know if I was mad, surprised, incredulous, or what. I did know one thing, I was ready to get fucked up. You see, whenever I got pissed off and wanted to push something out of my mind, or found myself powerless over a situation that I desperately wanted to control, it was time to get high, time for escapism.

On the way to Woodrow's crib I stopped and bought two forty ounce Colt 45's, the suds of choice, and a pack of Top rolling papers. I had weed and so did Woodrow. When I got there he had just finished eating.

"My man Lamont comin' with the Forty right on time," he said locking the door behind me. "What up Homie?"

"Man, JT and Sugar is hangin' out."

He looked at me blankly. "Didn't I just tell you that last night fool?"

"Yeah man, but I saw JT's car around the corner at the shooting gallery."

"What shooting gallery," he said as he cracked the cap on a Forty.

"You remember that time me and JT went with Sugar to do some hustlin?"

"Yeah," said Wood leaning forward.

"Well, that night he took us to a building around the corner on forty-third street where there were a bunch of dudes firing drugs."

"Ya'll did it too?"

"Hell naw, Sugar did, but JT is there now." Woodrow took another major swig from his bottle, sat it on the cocktail table, and pulled out a fat sack of weed. "I'm gettin' ready to get high, you can go around there and play Father Flanagan if you want to."

"Naw, I'm just sayin'," my eyes pleading to no avail; he kept on rolling. So we smoked, drank, and pissed until eight o'clock that night.

"Yo Lamont, I need to go down to the spot and check my traps. You want to roll?" "Let's do it," I replied bubbly.

When we got down to the jects the first thing the guy working the door said was, "Duh Duh been callin' here all day for you Woody."

"Good, that punk must have my money." Woodrow turned all business then, even though we were both drunk off our ass. "Did he say where he was?"

"Naw man, but he did say he was comin' down here."

"Give me the paper so I can get that out of the way," Wood ordered. The worker reached under the T.V. cart and pulled out a huge wad of money and handed it over. "Come on Lamont and help me count this jack."

"Okay," I said as I took off my coat, licked my fingers, and proceeded to count money at the kitchen table.

Just as we finished there was a knock at the back door. Wood quickly gave the money to one of the guys who left the room. Another worker looked through the peephole and said, "It's Duh Duh."

"Hold on," said Woodrow, "I'm going out in the hall. Come on Lamont." I grabbed my coat and followed Woodrow on out. Duh Duh looked surprised when Woodrow didn't ask him in, but instead backed up with a look of dejected resignation.

"What's up Wood? Hey Lamont," he said with a look of defeat. I could tell he didn't have Wood's money. Woodrow cut right into him like a viper.

"Man fuck all that, where's my money?"

"I'm hurtin' man," lamented Duh Duh.

"Not as hurt as you gon' be mutha fucka. You best be comin' out of your pockets with somethin' I ain't bullshitin'." Duh Duh simply shook his head from side to side as if he wasn't even hearing Woodrow. He was shuffling his feet and wringing his hands and looking seriously disturbed.

"What's wrong Duh Duh?" I asked.

"Everything man, everything," he answered, as a thin stream of saliva ran down from the corner of his mouth.

"Man what are you on?" shouted Woodrow.

"She left me man," blubbered Duh Duh as he wiped his mouth with the back of his trembling hand. "I did everything man, goddamn I did everything! She still left me for another dude, some pretty mutha fucka from the west side."

Woodrow didn't want to hear Duh Duh's wailing. "That wasn't even a real bitch you fool!"

"Don't say that!" screamed Duh Duh lunging at Woodrow as if to choke him. I quickly grabbed Duh Duh and pulled him back, which wasn't easy because Duh Duh was not only bigger than me, but he was on something which only made him harder to control.
"Leave him alone!" came a shout from the flight of stairs below. It was JT, who looked terrible stumbling up from the darkness.

"Ain't nobody done nothin to him yet," shouted Woodrow. "Anyway he owe me money."

"Fuck money, fuck that bitch, fuck you, fuck everything," cried Duh Duh, loosing it more by the minute.

"Oh you gon' pay me goddamit," threatened Woodrow.

"Or what, . . or what Wood, you gon' kill me? I'm already dead hell," wailed Duh Duh through a deluge of tears.

"Not all the way bitch," snapped Woodrow as he lunged toward Duh Duh pummeling him with a barrage of blows. JT stumbled into the fray beating Woodrow in the back of his head with his fists.

That's when I saw it, with IT being everything. It took all of JT's strength to raise his arms above his head in a feeble attempt to strike Woodrow. His fists trembled like an old frail invalid desperately trying to get his body to do what the mind had asked. I could see months of dirt packed under his fingernails as his pupils moved from side to side in a valiant effort to focus on Woody. It was pathetic and heartbreaking. That's when I realized IT was all over . . . IT being everything.

"JT!" I shouted as I grabbed him by the back of his coat collar. He went tumbling down the stairs like a rag doll. I couldn't believe this was the same JT who was our leader, our rock. When I looked back at Duh Duh and Woodrow I could see that Duh Duh wasn't really fighting back. He had his hands down by his sides letting Wood beat the shit out of him. JT was at the bottom of the stairs in a senseless heap and I was torn between helping him or Duh Duh. I chose Duh Duh.

"Don't stop, don't stop goddamit I want to die," cried Duh Duh as I half dragged and half begged Woodrow to stop beating him.

"Come on Wood," I pleaded, can't you see he ain't gon' fight you back?" Woodrow exhausted and half out of breath could hardly speak.

"Take yo' retarded ass back to yo' auntie's house mutha fucka and don't be comin' round here you worthless fag!"

"I can't, she don't want me no mo," sobbed Duh Duh through a flood of tears, snot, and saliva. "She say I can't show my face before God because I'm a heathen and a dope fiend."

"Just think if she knew you was sleepin' with a man," stabbed Woodrow. "She'd really be through with yo' ass!" That was it. That was the straw that broke Duh

Duh's back. He sprawled face down on the hallway floor, his body heaving with convulsed spasms.

"I know, I know! ... I couldn't help myself, nobody ever gave a fuck about me except her. Oh God I hated myself but I loved her!"

We watched him lay there sobbing so heavily I thought he'd choke. "I hope you're proud of yourself." It was JT laying at the foot of the stairs looking as though he'd been tumbled in a dryer. His bloodshot eyes were sunk way back in his head, his fists all swollen from dope needle misses.

"You should really feel fuckin' good now Woody," JT stammered through labored breaths. "We all knew the deal but where else was he gon' go? He ain't got no momma, he ain't got no daddy, we all he got you stupid dick! Now look what you done did." I slid down the wall and squatted with my face in my hands wishing I could push myself out of there and back to 1972.

What happened to that adventurous group of boys that liked practical jokes and softball? We had avoided gangs and jail and all that bad stuff so that we could end up here in this putrid hallway? Woodrow, once the prince of the neighborhood now a bitter dope dealer with no way out. Duh Duh, a guy with problems yes, but as innocent and lovable as a teddy bear slumped at my feet in the throes of an apparent nervous breakdown. JT, once our proud leader now barreling down the super-highway to a wretched reckoning. And me, at the crossroads knowing full well that I'd have to leave that hallway and never return.

Woodrow's door opened and the worker stuck his head out. "Everything cool Woody?"

"Yeah D.C., everything's cool," came Wood's defeated reply. Just then Duh Duh began to drag himself up.

"Where you goin?" I asked. No answer. I looked at Woodrow, my eyes pleading for him to say something, anything. Nothing. On the way by Duh Duh grabbed my hand and squeezed it real hard. "Where you goin' Duh Duh?" I pleaded once again, the tears streaming down his face. "I'll go with you," I offered as I attempted to rise. He pushed me back down and started down the stairs. When he reached JT he helped his childhood hero, protector, and friend to his feet then held him in his arms as he began to weep afresh.

When he turned and began to walk down the steps JT looked after him and softly said, "See you."

Duh Duh walked out into the bitter cold Chicago winter like a zombie. He was unaffected by the frigid, swirling two degree winds. He didn't care anymore. He went around to the yard where he'd played so many games of hide-and-go-seek, took his key out and went into the super clean hallway he had scrubbed so many times before and up the stairs he had counted and knew by heart. This time he didn't stop at twenty-eight steps. He rubbed his door with his finger as he went by and continued to the fourth floor. When he got there he took off his coat and laid it neatly on the floor. He took off all his clothes sobbing quietly and laid them in a neat pile below the window. Then he opened the window, stepped out onto the ledge, closed his eyes, and leaned forward.

After a few days it became evident the housing authority wasn't going to remove the bloodstained snow at Duh Duh's door, so me and my brother took the shovels we used to dig out snowed in cars and got it up. I started crying while we worked and as I look back on that moment my brother showed unusual maturity by letting me get it all out.

Duh Duh's funeral was sad. His aunt was there. Everybody in the neighborhood was there, except JT. I kept turning around every time the door squeaked to see if it was him but it wasn't. Woodrow at first seemed to be taking it kinda hard until Ervin walked in with his mother who no one could ever remember seeing.

"There go Duh Duh's daddy," whispered Woodrow. I tried to hold my laugh, but after snot shot out of my nose from the pressure I had to let it go. When Woody saw this we guffawed right there in the front row of Duh Duh's funeral. It was so embarrassing. Then Ervin hippity-hopped up to look in the casket and we couldn't hold the reprise. By then everybody knew we were laughing at Ervin and we couldn't stop. It was really messed up. We had hopped L's together, climbed roofs, and played some of the most serious games of catch-one-catch-'em all you could imagine. But here at the end it was him being feeble-minded that we fondly remembered. We were still kids.

A TURKEY IN SUSPENSE

Charles Allen Woods had no idea what Papa D. dealt with on a daily: soldiers, like hyenas hoping to get an extra package by mistake, coming in with short trap at the end of the day with all kinds of excuses, the doctor on the North side who they had been buying scripts for Robitussin AC from wants Wood to call him (no doubt to ask for more money . . . again), and of course Darlene is always in his ear,
, "Woody, this is the guitar I need so that when I finish my Far East Acupuncture class I can move right into jazz guitar that same week."

"Girl why can't you just go to school for one thing like everybody else instead of all this goofball shit you be comin up with?" Wood was developing rings around his eyes, a permanent furrow across his brow, and a pronounced scowl.

"Woody, manners are learned but class is bred. All those dance classes are why I move ladylike with grace and shit, and I'm sure I don't have to explain my fashion sense to you. I'm gonna be something, and I'm gonna go someplace other than this shithole you call the spot. Daddy understood that and he was all about us being something."

The daddy reference took Wood over the top. "Oh yeah, then what the fuck am I gon' be Darlene? Where are my fucking classes? Dope fiend mutha fuckas trying me on a daily, Jo Jo not lifting a goddamn finger other than to eat up all the dope he possibly can, and everybody else including you with their hand out begging for something. When can I go get some Acu-Fucking-Puncture! "

"I'll come back," Darlene popped spritely as she jumped from her seat and left the room. She, like everyone else couldn't see Woodrow. All they saw was the spot, the dope house, the fence, the shylock commerce center, and the community overlord whose benevolence was omnipresent and all encompassing. Woodrow had no idea who his father was until he died and Butch moved to Cleveland to live with her sister. Pressure either made diamonds or burst pipes. There was no middle ground where Wood could bask on 31st Street Beach or hang out in Grant Park with the little honeys his fame had produced.

The pressure on Woodrow was palpable. He'd aged five years in 365 days with the holiday season of 1975 being the galvanizing apex of his reign as the young prince. He and I were outside the spot smoking a Kool (I hated cigarettes) while Sugar was at his hallway post trying his best to look sentry-like and inconspicuous at the same time. "Sooooo, what happened with the turkeys?" I asked, trying to be as non-accusatory as I could.

"Ain't shit happened with 'em," spit Wood equally non-chalant, "I forgot."

"Nigga you ain't forgot," I spat back. "Just say fuck 'em like you done everything else, but don't insult me or yourself with that bullshit." Wood took a deep drag on his square and let the smoke escape as if he had just tapped out in a wrestling match,   "Yeah well fuck them toys too." He was referring to the twenty plus year tradition of Papa D's giving Christmas toys to damn near every Ida B. Wells apartment from Thirty-ninth to Thirty-seventh. It was a huge, expensive, giant hearted event that everybody from the kids and the parents to the J.T.'s and the soldiers who made the deliveries looked forward to.

I remember one Christmas I knocked on a door and this dude answered with needles stuck in BOTH arms! I nearly jumped out of my skin. To this day I don't remember what he looked like because all I could see was those needles hanging out of his arms. They were hospital kinda needles, not street spikes put together with rubber bands and tape. And he had those rubber straps around each arm like they use in hospitals. I figured if you're poppin in the comfort of your home you probably had an upgraded outfit.

"This that fire and ice," he announced proudly. I knew instantly what he was talking about. He was shooting a speedball . . . cocaine in one arm and heroin in the other. Looking at his needles closely I could see that the brew in the left arm was golden colored. Heroin. The brew in the right arm was pale like urine. Coke. This fool was showing off. I bet hearing that knock on the door gave him a rush and he couldn't wait to display his arts (after checking the peep-hole of course).

He had muscular arms with big fat veins poppin' out of 'em and a dingy wife beater on. I started to hand him his box with the turkey in it but I could tell he didn't want to bend his arms and I was right.

"Sit it on that table shorty," he gestured. I went in and sat the box down and made a beeline for the door. "Aight lil Homie," he said triumphantly knowing he'd sufficiently rocked my world.

I remember one time this fine mama answered a door on the third floor. Her kids snatched the presents with a little squeal and ran in the house leaving me and mama standing at the door staring each other down. She had a drink in her hand. "Damn young blood you kinda cute," she purred. I don't know how old she was, maybe late twenties, early thirties; I was 16, tops.

"You lookin good too, " I stammered.

A few seconds passed as she swayed in the doorway, then she said, "Come here," then grabbed me by the collar, pulled me in close to her body, and laid the first super open- mouthed, gangster tongue kiss on me I had ever had. Then she pushed me out in the hall and slammed the door. I stood there stunned for a minute with a big goofy smile then stumbled downstairs to the welcoming brisk winter blast on my face. For years every time I went past that hallway I looked up at the window hoping she'd stick her head out and give me a wink.

"Wood, yo daddy built everything ya'll got on his relationship with Ida B. These people love him and you because of that. It's one thing to call in your debts, hell, people know they owe that money, but it's a whole other thing to destroy a tradition older than you.There's a lot of talk going around about how you ain't your daddy, and how you fuckin' up the business, and how Squeaky gon' take over and shit like that."

Wood exploded. "I don't give a FUCK what these niggas sayin. I didn't sign up for this BULLSHIT, this shit was dropped in my lap and you know what? I'm liquidating all this shit anyway. I'm gon' open me a gas station and go legit, FUCK 'em!"

I looked at him as if I could see into the marrow of his bones and said flatly, "Really." He took the last pull off his square, flicked it as hard and as far as he could. Silence.

No turkeys went out on Thanksgiving and no toys on Christmas that year. It was the worst Christmas I could remember in the projects. I avoided the spot, I avoided Wood's brownstone, I avoided people in the hood cause all they wanted to talk about was "Ya boy Wood."

Even my Mama had something to say. "The neighborhood is mighty unhappy about not getting them turkeys, for real. There are some girlfriends of mine up on Thirty-ninth who say they ain't lookin out or making no more phone calls if the police come through."

"Why?" I questioned.

"They've been getting turkeys for over twenty years, now they're gonna go crazy cause he missed one year." She looked at me as if I didn't understand (which I didn't). "Most everybody around here is on welfare, they plan their holiday shopping knowing they'll get turkey dinners and toys to help 'em out. He messed up a whole lot of Christmases."

I took a deep sigh because I knew she was right. Wood should've taken a step back and more accurately assessed the situation. These people were his protection. Papa D would have never done anything like that

IN A TWINKLE

The next day we found out JT had OD'd in an old tenement on forty-third street. Disco Mix came around and told me. I went in the bathroom and cried. Then I took a hot bath. My mother kept coming to the door asking if I was alright, which I acknowledged in monosyllabic affirmation. This was it. I'll never forget it for as long as I live. That day in the tub I made up my mind to do something with my life. I was going to graduate in June and I began to wonder which one of those colleges from the catalogues might take me. I had to leave the projects. I kept re-heating my bath with fresh hot water as I contemplated my plan which definitely needed some serious contemplation seeing as how I was number 286 out of a graduating class of 364. I figured that was better than Dino; he was dead. It was better than Duh Duh and JT, because they were dead too. Raimey Boy had dropped out and was working at some tire shop, and Stevie D. was in jail for possession.

It's funny how major events in one's life come on with the suddenness of a thunderstorm. There are warning flashes that we either do nothing about or chose to ignore. Then there is the cool cloudiness of impending doom that always rolls in much too fast. So we try to get all of our fun in before we take shelter or once again hope it passes by leaving us unscathed. By the time we feel the pelting reality of life stinging us it's too late. We're drenched in change whether we like it or not.

That was me in the bathtub. Soaked in the permutation of all the different paths I could've taken and finally admitting I'd been in a low-pressure system my whole life. I guess I hoped it would rain on the other side of the street.

THE YOUNG PRINCE

Three days after New Years on January fourth 1976 the police raided the spot. Woodrow was there. There were burglar bars on the doors so they had to knock those in with heavy hammers or something. I wasn't there by some fortuitous happenstance because like I said, I'd kinda distanced myself from that unpopular place. The talk about Squeaky and his gang takin' over had really picked up so I guess that's what Wood must've been thinking when he ran in the kitchen and got the gun, even though I heard the men were shouting "POLICE" all over the place. Maybe Wood was getting high and not in his right mind when he aimed at the front door and pulled the trigger. Maybe he was in a panic and just lost himself completely as he continued firing until the revolver was empty. Maybe he thought he'd run Squeaky's ass off once and for all. But that wasn't the case. He'd shot a cop in the face and it was bad, really bad. There was so much shooting and blood that they never rented that apartment again.

Somehow Woodrow miraculously lived through the nightmare with a few bullet holes in him. He'd lost a leg but he wasn't going anywhere. Life without the possibility of parole for attempted murder of a police officer. He shouldda gave out them turkeys.

EPILOGUE

There was a great swing set in Madden Park. It was built of pure steel to last fifty years. The seats were thick wood and the ropes were strong chain link. We'd stand on the seat part and pump ourselves so high into the sky we nearly went over the top. At the highest point possible we'd sit on the back-swoop and when the swing came forward we'd bail out like daredevil paratroopers flying high and far into the air. There was a fence that you could slide into if you were skilled and daring enough to go for it. Also in the park were two huge sandboxes where we'd play "Root The Peg." It was a game played with a screwdriver (poor kids made great games up out of seemingly nothing) where you'd flip the screwdriver off your knuckles, elbows, shoulders, and even your head in an attempt to make it stick straight up in the sand. Believe it or not there were kids who could flip that screwdriver with such dexterity it'd make you dizzy! We'd swim in the pool all day and then run our rusty, shriveled up, chlorinated behinds to Mr. Quinn the candy man and buy duplex sandwich cookies and Jay's

Potato Chips. We played until we were delirious. And when we got older we all took puffs off our mother's cigarettes when they sent us into the kitchen to light them. We were all the same and yet, we were all different, most times by the most innocuous distinction.

Woodrow, JT, Duh Duh, and Dino all went to Doolittle. I went to Mayo Elementary named after them doctors.

No matter what I did after school in the projects, between 8am and 3:15 I was immersed. I had a different foundation than the guys I hung out with. I was passing classes as we sneaked into concerts while they struggled to read at grade level. That was never discussed, not in the projects, because you got beat up if you were a smarty-pants. The most profound element of this whole scenario was that I wasn't supposed to go to Mayo. Project kids went to Doolittle.

My mother lied about my address.

After all my friends were gone I went to this educational service where people helped you apply to colleges, take SATs, and get financial aide and stuff. It was called Ada S. McKinley and it was located in the basement of the Dearborn Homes Projects. I don't know how I found out about it; I'm thinking the ghost of Brenda Oglesby took me there. I sat for the ACT and scored pretty good on it. I applied to Grambling, Jackson State (because Walter Payton went there), and Henderson State University in Arkansas. Jackson State offered me an academic scholarship so I went there. I remember walking onto the campus from the train station in 1976 and seeing a big banner strung across the entrance. "Welcome to Jackson State University – Brick House Country."

I never went back to my projects. I heard there's an upscale grocery store where my building used to be with white folks living in condos, walking poodles and shit, and the last President of the United States, a **BLACK MAN** has a house a few blocks away. Damn.